CITY OF THE DREADFUL NIGHT

THE CITY OF DREADFUL NIGHT

BY
RUDYARD
KIPLING

Fredonia Books
Amsterdam, The Netherlands

The City of Dreadful Night

by
Rudyard Kipling

ISBN 1-58963-259-1

Reprinted from the Original edition

Fredonia Books
Amsterdam, The Netherlands
http://www.fredoniabooks.com

In order to make original editions of historical works available to scholars at an economical price, this facsimile of the original edition is reproduced from the best available copy and has been digitally enhanced to improve legibility, but the text remains unaltered to retain historical authenticity.

CONTENTS

CHAPTER I

A REAL LIVE CITY

WE are all backwoodsmen and barbarians together—we others dwelling beyond the Ditch, in the outer darkness of the Mofussil. There are no such things as commissioners and heads of departments in the world, and there is only one city in India. Bombay is too green, too pretty and too stragglesome; and Madras died ever so long ago. Let us take off our hats to Calcutta, the many-sided, the smoky, the magnificent, as we drive in over the Hugli Bridge in the dawn of a still February morning. We have left India behind us at Howrah Station, and now we enter foreign parts. No, not wholly foreign. Say rather too familiar.

All men of certain age know the feeling of caged irritation—an illustration in the *Graphic*, a bar of music of the light words of a friend from home may set it ablaze—that comes from the knowledge of our lost heritage of London. At home they, the other men, our equals, have at their disposal all that town can supply—the roar of the streets, the lights, the music, the pleasant places, the millions of their own kind, and a wilderness full of pretty, fresh-colored Englishwomen, theatres and restaurants. It is their right. They accept it as such, and even affect to look upon it with contempt. And we, we have nothing except the few amusements that we painfully build up for ourselves—the dolorous dissipations of gymkhanas where every one knows everybody else, or the chastened intoxication of dances where all engagements are booked, in ink, ten days ahead, and where everybody's antecedents are as patent as his or her method of waltzing. We have been deprived of our inheritance. The men at home are enjoying it all, not knowing how fair and rich it is, and we at the most can only fly westward for a few months and gorge what, properly speaking, should take seven or eight or ten luxurious years. That is the lost heritage of London; and the knowledge of the forfeiture, wilful or forced, comes to most men at times and seasons, and they get cross.

Calcutta holds out false hopes of some return. The dense smoke hangs low, in the chill of the morning, over an ocean of roofs, and, as the city wakes, there goes up to the smoke a deep, full-throated boom of life and motion and humanity. For this reason does he who sees Calcutta for the first time hang joyously out of the *ticca-gharri* and sniff the smoke. and turn his face toward the tumult, saying: "This is, at last, some portion of my heritage returned to me. This is a city. There is life here, and there should be all manner of pleasant things for the having, across the river and under the smoke." When Leland, he who wrote the Hans Breitmann Ballads, once desired to know the name of an austere, plug-hatted red-skin of repute, his answer, from the lips of a half-bred, was:

"He Injun. He big Injun. He heap big Injun. He dam big heap Injun. He dam mighty great big heap Injun. He Jones!" The litany is an expressive one, and exactly describes the first emotions of a wandering savage adrift in Calcutta. The eye has lost its sense of proportion, the focus has contracted through overmuch residence in up-country stations—twenty minutes' canter from hospital to parade-ground, you know—and the mind has shrunk with the eye. Both say together, as they take in the sweep of shipping above and below the Hugli Bridge: "Why, this is London! This is the docks. This is Imperial. This is worth coming across India to see!"

Then a distinctly wicked idea takes possession of the mind: "What a divine—what a heavenly place to *loot!*" This gives place to a much worse devil—that of Conservatism. It seems not only a wrong but a criminal thing to allow natives to have any voice in the control of such a city—adorned, docked, wharfed, fronted and reclaimed by Englishmen, existing only because England lives, and dependent for its life on England. All India knows of the Calcutta Municipality; but has any one thoroughly investigated the Big Calcutta Stink? There is only one. Benares is fouler in point of concentrated, pent-up muck, and there are local stenches in Peshawur which are stronger than the B. C. S.; but, for diffused, soul-sickening expansiveness, the reek of Calcutta beats both Benares and Peshawur. Bombay cloaks her stenches with a veneer of assafœtida and *huqa*-tobacco; Calcutta is above pretence. There is no tracing back the Calcutta plague to any one source. It is faint, it is sickly, and it is indescribable; but Americans at the Great Eastern Hotel say that it is something like the smell of the Chinese quarter in San Francisco. It is certainly not an Indian smell. It resembles the essence of corruption that has rotted for the second time—the clammy odor of blue slime. And there is no escape from it. It blows across the *maidan;* it comes in gusts into the corridors of the Great Eastern Hotel; what they are pleased to call the "Palaces of Chouringhi" carry it; it swirls round the Bengal Club; it pours out of by-streets with sickening intensity, and the breeze of the morning is laden with it. It is first found, in spite of the fume of the engines, in Howrah Station. It seems to be worst in the little lanes at the back of Lal Bazar where the drinking-shops are, but it is nearly as bad opposite Government House and in the Public Offices. The thing is intermittent. Six moderately pure mouthfuls of air may be drawn without offence. Then comes the seventh wave and the queasiness of an uncultured stomach. If you live long enough in Calcutta you grow used to it. The regular residents admit the disgrace, but their answer is: "Wait till the wind blows off the Salt Lakes where all the sewage goes, and *then* you'll smell something." That is their defence! Small wonder that they consider Calcutta is a fit place for a permanent Viceroy. Englishmen who can calmly extenuate one shame by another are capable of asking for anything—and expecting to get it.

If an up-country station holding three thousand troops and twenty civilians owned such a possession as Calcutta does, the Deputy Commissioner or the Cantonment Magistrate would have all the natives off the board of management or decently shoveled into the background until the mess was abated. Then they might come on again and talk of "high-handed oppression" as much as they liked. That stink, to an unprejudiced nose, damns Calcutta as a City of Kings.

And, in spite of that stink, they allow, they even encourage, natives to look after the place! The damp, drainage-soaked soil is sick with the teeming life of a hundred years, and the Municipal Board list is choked with the names of natives—men of the breed born in and raised off this surfeited muck-heap! They own property, these amiable Aryans on the Municipal and the Bengal Legislative Council. Launch a proposal to tax them on that property, and they naturally howl. They also howl up-country, but there the halls for mass-meetings are few, and the vernacular papers fewer, and with a *zubbardusti* Secretary and a President whose favor is worth the having and whose wrath is undesirable, men are kept clean despite themselves, and may not poison their neighbors. Why, asks a savage, let them vote at all? They can put up with this filthiness. They *cannot* have any feelings worth caring a rush for. Let them live quietly and hide away their money under our protection, while we tax them till they know through their purses the measure of their neglect in the past, and when a little of the smell has been abolished, bring them back again to talk and take the credit of enlightenment. The better classes own their broughams and barouches; the worse can shoulder an Englishman into the kennel and talk to him as though he were a *khitmatgar*. They can refer to an English lady as an *aurat;* they are permitted a freedom—not to put it too coarsely—of speech which, if used by an Englishman toward an Englishman, would end in serious trouble. They are fenced and protected and made inviolate. Surely they might be content with all those things without entering into matters which they cannot, by the nature of their birth, understand.

Now, whether all this genial diatribe be the outcome of an unbiased mind or the result first of sickness caused by that ferocious stench, and secondly of headache due to day-long smoking to drown the stench, is an open question. Anyway, Calcutta is a fearsome place for a man not educated up to it.

A word of advice to other barbarians. Do not bring a north-country servant into Calcutta. He is sure to get into trouble, because he does not understand the customs of the city. A Punjabi in this place for the first time esteems it his bounden duty to go to the *Ajaib-ghar*—the Museum. Such an one has gone and is even now returned very angry and troubled in the spirit. "I went to the Museum," says he, "and no one gave me any *gali.* I went to the market to buy my food, and then I sat upon a seat. There came a *chaprissi* who said: 'Go away, I want to sit here.' I said: 'I am here first.' He said: 'I am a *chaprissi! nikal jao!*' and he hit me. Now that sitting-place was open to all, so I hit him till he wept. He ran away for the Police, and I went away too, for the Police here are all *Sahibs*. Can I have leave from two o'clock to go and look for that *chaprissi* and hit him again?"

Behold the situation! An unknown city full of smell that makes one long for rest and retirement, and a champing *naukar*, not yet six hours in the stew, who has started a blood-feud with an unknown *chaprissi* and clamors to go forth to the fray. General orders that, whatever may be said or done to him, he must not say or do anything in return lead to an eloquent harangue on the quality of *izzat* and the nature of "face blackening." There is no *izzat* in Calcutta, and this Awful Smell blackens the face of any Englishman who sniffs it.

Alas! for the lost delusion of the heritage that was to be restored. Let us sleep, let us sleep, and pray that Calcutta may be better to-morrow.

At present it is remarkably like sleeping with a corpse.

CHAPTER II

THE REFLECTIONS OF A SAVAGE

MORNING brings counsel. *Does* Calcutta smell so pestiferously after all? Heavy rain has fallen in the night. She is newly-washed, and the clear sunlight shows her at her best. Where, oh where, in all this wilderness of life shall a man go? Newman and Co. publish a three-rupee guide which produces first despair and then fear in the mind of the reader. Let us drop Newman and Co. out of the topmost window of the Great Eastern, trusting to luck and the flight of the hours to evolve wonders and mysteries and amusements.

The Great Eastern hums with life through all its hundred rooms. Doors slam merrily, and all the nations of the earth run up and down the staircases. This alone is refreshing, because the passers bump you and ask you to stand aside. Fancy finding any place outside a Levée-room where Englishmen are crowded together to this extent! Fancy sitting down seventy strong to *tâble d'hôte* and with a deafening clatter of knives and forks! Fancy finding a real bar whence drinks may be obtained! and, joy of joys, fancy stepping out of the hotel into the arms of a live, white, helmeted, buttoned, truncheoned Bobby! A beautiful, burly Bobby—just the sort of man who, seven thousand miles away, staves off the stuttering witticism of the three-o'clock-in-the-morning reveler by the strong badged arm of authority. What would happen if one spoke to this Bobby? Would he be offended? He is not offended. He is affable. He has to patrol the pavement in front of the Great Eastern and to see that the crowding *ticca-gharris* do not jam. Toward a presumably respectable white he behaves as a man and a brother. There is no arrogance about him. And this is disappointing. Closer inspection shows that he is not a *real* Bobby after all. He is a Municipal Police something and his uniform is not correct; at least if they have not changed the dress of the men at home. But no matter. Later on we will inquire into the Calcutta Bobby, because he is a white man, and has to deal with some of the "toughest" folk that ever set out of malice aforethought to paint Job Charnock's city vermillion. You must not, you cannot cross Old Court House Street without looking carefully to see that you stand no chance of being run over. This is beautiful. There is a steady roar of traffic, cut every two minutes by the deeper roll of the trams.

The driving is eccentric, not to say bad, but there is the traffic—more that unsophisticated eyes have beheld for a certain number of years. It means business, it means money-making, it means crowded and hurrying life, and it gets into the blood and makes it move. Here be big shops with plate-glass fronts—all displaying the well-known names of firms that we savages only correspond with through the V. P. P. and Parcels Post. They are all here, as large as life, ready to supply anything you need if you only care to sign. Great is the fascination of being able to obtain a thing on the spot without having to write for a week and wait for a month, and then get something quite different. No wonder pretty ladies, who live anywhere within a reasonable distance, come down to do their shopping personally.

"Look here. If you want to be respectable you mustn't smoke in the streets. Nobody does it." This is advice kindly tendered by a friend in a black coat. There is no Levée or Lieutenant-Governor in sight; but he wears the frock-coat because it is daylight, and he can be seen. He also refrains from smoking for the same reason. He admits that Providence built the open air to be smoked in, but he says that "it isn't the thing." This man has a brougham, a remarkably natty little pill-box with a curious wabble about the wheels. He steps into the brougham and puts on—a top hat, a shiny black "plug."

There was a man up-country once who owned a top-hat. He leased it to amateur theatrical companies for some seasons until the nap wore off. Then he threw it into a tree and wild bees hived in it. Men were wont to come and look at the hat, in its palmy days, for the sake of feeling homesick. It interested all the station, and died with two seers of *babul* flower honey in its bosom. But top-hats are not intended to be worn in India. They are as sacred as home letters and old rosebuds. The friend cannot see this. He allows that if he stepped out of his brougham and walked about in the sunshine for ten minutes he would get a bad headache. In half-an-hour he would probably catch sunstroke. He allows all this, but he keeps to his hat and cannot see why a barbarian is moved to inextinguishable laughter at the sight. Every one who owns a brougham and many people who hire *ticca-gharris* keep top-hats and black frock-coats. The effect is curious, and at first fills the beholder with surprise.

And now, "let us see the handsome houses where the wealthy nobles dwell." Northerly lies the great human jungle of the native city, stretching from Burra Bazar to Chitpore. That can keep. Southerly is the *maidan* and Chouringhi.

"If you get out into the centre of the *maidan* you will understand why Calcutta is called the City of Palaces." The traveled American said so at the Great Eastern. There is a short tower, falsely called a "memorial," standing in a waste of soft, sour green. That is as good a place to get to as any other. Near here the newly-landed waler is taught the whole duty of the trap-horse and careers madly in a brake. Near here young Calcutta gets upon a horse and is incontinently run away with. Near here hundreds of kine feed, close to the innumerable trams and the whirl of traffic along the face of Chouringhi Road. The size of the *maidan* takes the heart out of any one accustomed to the "gardens" of up-country, just as they say Newmarket Heath cows a horse accustomed to more shut-in course. The huge level is studded with brazen statues of eminent gentlemen riding fretful horses on diabolically severe curbs. The expanse dwarfs the statues, dwarfs everything except the frontage of the far-away Chouringhi Road. It is big—it is impressive. There is no escaping the fact. They built houses in the old days when the rupee was two shillings and a penny. Those houses are three-storied, and ornamented with service-staircases like houses in the Hills. They are also very close together, and they own garden walls of *pukka*-masonry pierced with a single gate. In their shut-upness they are British. In their spaciousness they are Oriental, but those service-stair-cases do not look healthy. We will form an amateur sanitary commission and call upon Chouringhi.

A first introduction to the Calcutta *durwan* is not nice. If he is chewing *pan,* he does not take the trouble to get rid of his quid. If he is sitting on his *charpoy* chewing sugarcane, he does not think it worth his while to rise. He has to be taught those things, and he cannot understand why he should be reproved. Clearly he is a survival of a played-out system. Providence never intended that any native should be made a *concierge* more insolent than any of the French variety. The people of Calcutta put an Uria in a little lodge close to the gate of their house, in order that loafers may be turned away, and the houses protected from theft. The natural result is that the *durwan* treats everybody whom he does not know as a loafer, has an intimate and vendible knowledge of all the outgoings and incomings in that house, and controls, to a large extent, the nomination of the *naukar-log.* They say that one of the estimable class is now suing a bank for about three lakhs of rupees. Up-country, a Lieutenant-Governor's *chaprissi* has to work for thirty years before he can retire on seventy thousand rupees of savings. The Calcutta *durwan* is a great institution. The head and front of his offence is that he will insist upon trying to talk English. How he protects the houses Calcutta only knows. He can be frightened out of his wits by severe speech, and is generally asleep in calling hours. If a rough round of visits be any guide, three times out of seven he is fragrant of drink. So much for the *durwan*. Now for the houses he guards.

Very pleasant is the sensation of being ushered into a pestiferously stablesome drawing-room. "Does this always happen?" "No, not unless you shut up the room for some time; but if you open the *jhilmills* there are other smells. You see the stables and the servants' quarters are close too." People pay five hundred a month for half-a-dozen rooms filled with *attr* of this kind. They make no complaint. When they think the honor of the city is at stake they say defiantly: "Yes, but you must remember we're a metropolis. We are crowded here. We have no room. We aren't like your little stations." Chouringhi is a stately place full of sumptuous houses, but it is best to look at it hastily. Stop to consider for a moment what the cramped compounds, the black soaked soil, the netted intricacies, of the service-staircases, the packed stables, the seethment of human life round the *durwans'* lodges and the curious arrangement of little open drains means, and you will call it a whited sepulchre.

Men living in expensive tenements suffer from chronic sore-throat, and will tell you cheerily that "we've got typhoid in Calcutta now." Is the pest ever out of it? Everything seems to be built with a view to its comfort. It can lodge comfortably on roofs, climb along from the gutter-pipe to piazza, or rise from sink to veranda and thence to the topmost story. But Calcutta says that all is sound and produces figures to prove it; at the same time admitting that healthy cut flesh will not readily heal. Further evidence may be dispensed with.

Here come pouring down Park Street on the *maidan* a rush of broughams, neat buggies, the lightest of gigs, trim office brownberrys, shining victorias, and a sprinkling of veritable hansom cabs. In the broughams sit men in top-hats. In the other carts, young men, all very much alike, and all immaculately turned out. A fresh stream from Chouringhi joins the Park Street detachment, and the two together stream away across the *maidan* toward the business quarter of the city. This is Calcutta going to office—the civilians to the Government Buildings and the young men to their firms and their blocks and their wharves. Here one sees that Calcutta has the best turn-out in the Empire. Horses and traps alike are enviably perfect, and—mark the touchstone of civilization—*the lamps are in the sockets.* This is distinctly refreshing. Once more we will take off our hats to Calcutta, the well-appointed, the luxurious. The country-bred is a rare beast here; his place is taken by the waler, and the waler, though a ruffian at heart, can be made to look like a gentleman. It would be indecorous as well as insane to applaud the winking harness, the perfectly lacquered panels, and the liveried *saises.* They show well in the outwardly fair roads shadowed by the Palaces.

How many sections of the complex society of the place do the carts carry? *Imprimis,* the Bengal Civilian who goes to Writers' Buildings and sits in a perfect office and speaks flippantly of "sending things into India," meaning thereby the Supreme Government. He is a great person, and his mouth is full of promotion-and-appointment "shop." Generally he is referred to as a "rising man." Calcutta seems full of "rising men." *Secondly,* the Government of India man, who wears a familiar Simla face, rents a flat when he is not up in the Hills, and is rational on the subject of the drawbacks of Calcutta. *Thirdly,* the man of the "firms," the pure non-official who fights under the banner of one of the great houses of the City, or for his own hand in a neat office, or dashes about Clive Street in a brougham doing "share work" or something of the kind. He fears not "Bengal," nor regards he "India." He swears impartially at both when their actions interfere with his operations. His "shop" is quite unintelligible. He is like the English city man with the chill off, lives well and entertains hospitably. In the old days he was greater than he is now, but still he bulks large. He is rational in so far that he will help the abuse of the Municipality, but womanish in his insistence on the excellencies of Calcutta. Over and above these who are hurrying to work are the various brigades, squads and detachments of the other interests. But they are sets and not sections, and revolve round Belvedere, Government House, and Fort William. Simla and Darjeeling claim them in the hot weather. Let them go. They wear top-hats and frock-coats.

It is time to escape from Chouringhi Road and get among the long-shore folk, who have no prejudices against tobacco, and who all use pretty nearly the same sort of hat.

CHAPTER III

THE COUNCIL OF THE GODS

He set up conclusions to the number of nine thousand seven hundred and sixty four . . . he went afterward to the Sorbonne, where he maintained argument against the theologians for the space of six weeks, from four o'clock in the morning till six in the evening, except for an interval of two hours to refresh themselves and take their repasts, and at this were present the greatest part of the lords of the court the masters of request, presidents, counsellors, those of the accompts, secretaries, advocates, and others; as also the sheriffs of the said town.—*Pantagruel.*

"THE Bengal Legislative Council is sitting now. You will find it in an octagonal wing of Writers' Buildings: straight across the *maidan*. It's worth seeing." "What are they sitting on?" "Municipal business. No end of a debate." So much for trying to keep low company. The long-shore loafers must stand over. Without doubt this Council is going to hang some one for the state of the City, and Sir Steuart Bayley will be chief executioner. One does not come across Councils every day.

Writers' Buildings are large. You can trouble the busy workers of half-a-dozen departments before you stumble upon the black-stained staircase that leads to an upper chamber looking out over a populous street. Wild *chaprissis* block the way. The Councillor Sahibs are sitting, but any one can enter. "To the right of the Lât Sahib's chair, and go quietly." Ill-mannered minion! Does he expect the awe-stricken spectator to prance in with a jubilant war-whoop or turn Catherine-wheels round that sumptuous octagonal room with the blue-domed roof? There are gilt capitals to the half pillars and an Egyptian patterned lotus-stencil makes the walls decorously gay. A thick piled carpet covers all the floor, and must be delightful in the hot weather. On a black wooden throne, comfortably cushioned in green leather, sits Sir Steuart Bayley, Ruler of Bengal. The rest are all great men, or else they would not be there. Not to know them argues oneself unknown. There are a dozen of them, and sit six aside at two slightly curved lines of beautifully polished desks. Thus Sir Steuart Bayley occupies the frog of a badly made horseshoe split at the toe. In front of him, at a table covered with books and pamphlets and papers, toils a secretary. There is a seat for the Reporters, and that is all. The place enjoys a chastened gloom, and its very atmosphere fills one with awe. This is the heart of Bengal, and uncommonly well upholstered. If the work matches the first-class furniture, the inkpots, the carpet, and the resplendent ceiling, there will be something worth seeing. But where is the criminal who is to be hanged for the stench that runs up and down Writers' Buildings staircases, for the rubbish heaps in the Chitpore Road, for the sickly savor of Chouringhi, for the dirty little tanks at the back of Belvedere, for the street full of smallpox, for the reeking gharri-stand outside the Great Eastern, for the state of the stone and dirt pavements, for the condition of the gullies of Shampooker, and for a hundred other things?

"This, I submit, is an artificial scheme in supersession of Nature's unit, the individual." The speaker is a slight, spare native in a flat hat-turban, and a black alpaca frock-coat. He looks like a *vakil* to the boot-heels, and, with his unvarying smile and regulated gesticulation, recalls memories of up-country courts. He never hesitates, is never at a loss for a word, and never in one sentence repeats himself. He talks and talks and talks in a level voice, rising occasionally half an octave when a point has to be driven home. Some of his periods sound very familiar. This, for instance, might be a sentence from the *Mirror:* "So much for the principle. Let us now examine how far it is supported by precedent." This sounds bad. When a fluent native is discoursing of "principles" and "precedents," the chances are that he will go on for some time. Moreover, where is the criminal, and what is all this talk about abstractions? They want shovels not sentiments, in this part of the world.

A friendly whisper brings enlightenment: "They are plowing through the Calcutta Municipal Bill—plurality of votes you know; here are the papers." And so it is! A mass of motions and amendments on matters relating to ward votes. Is *A* to be allowed to give two votes in one ward and one in another? Is section ten to be omitted, and is one man to be allowed one vote and no more? How many votes does three hundred rupees' worth of landed property carry? Is it better to kiss a post or throw it in the fire? Not a word about carbolic acid and gangs of *domes*. The little man in the black *choga* revels in his subject. He is great on principles and precedents, and the necessity of "popularizing our system." He fears that under certain circumstances "the status of the candidates will decline." He riots in "self-adjusting majorities," and the healthy influence of the educated middle classes.

For a practical answer to this, there steals across the council chamber just one faint whiff. It is as though some one laughed low and bitterly. But no man heeds. The Englishmen look supremely bored, the native members stare stolidly in front of them. Sir Steuart Bayley's face is as set as the face of the Sphinx. For these things he draws his pay, and his is a low wage for heavy labor. But the speaker, now adrift, is not altogether to be blamed. He is a Bengali, who has got before him just such a subject as his soul loveth—an elaborate piece of academical reform leading no-whither. Here is a quiet room full of pens and papers, and there are men who must listen to him. Apparently there is no time limit to the speeches. Can you wonder that he talks? He says "I submit" once every ninety seconds, varying the form with "I do submit." The popular element in the electoral body should have prominence. Quite so. He quotes one John Stuart Mill to prove it. There steals over the listener a numbing sense of nightmare. He has heard all this before somewhere—yea; even down to J. S. Mill and the references to the "true interests of the ratepayers." He sees what is coming next. Yes, there is the old Sabha Anjuman journalistic formula—"Western education is an exotic plant of recent importation." How on earth did this man drag Western education into this discussion? Who knows? Perhaps Sir Steuart Bayley does. He seems to be listening. The others are looking at their watches. The spell of the level voice sinks the listener yet deeper into a trance. He is haunted by the ghosts of all the cant of all the political platforms of Great Britain. He hears all the old, old vestry phrases, and once more he smells the smell. *That* is no dream. Western education is an exotic plant. It is the upas tree, and it is all our fault. We brought it out from England exactly as we brought out the ink bottles and the patterns for the chairs. We planted it and it grew—monstrous as a banian. Now we are choked by the roots of it spreading so thickly in this fat soil of Bengal. The speaker continues. Bit by bit. We builded this dome, visible and invisible, the crown of Writers' Buildings, as we have built and peopled the buildings. Now we have gone too far to retreat, being "tied and bound with the chain of our own sins. "The speech continues. We made that florid sentence. That torrent of verbiage is ours. We taught him what was constitutional and what was unconstitutional in the days when Calcutta smelt. Calcutta smells still, but we must listen to all that he has to say about the plurality of votes and the threshing of wind and the weaving of ropes of sand. It is our own fault absolutely.

The speech ends, and there rises a grey Englishman in a black frock-coat. He looks a strong man, and a worldly. Surely he will say: "Yes, Lala Sahib, all this may be true talk, but there's a *burra krab* smell in this place, and everything must be *safkaroed* in a week, or the Deputy

Commissioner will not take any notice of you in *durbar*." He says nothing of the kind. This is a Legislative Council, where they call each other "Honorable So-and-So's." The Englishman in the frock-coat begs all to remember that "we are discussing principles, and no consideration of the details ought to influence the verdict on the principles." Is he then like the rest? How does this strange thing come about? Perhaps these so English office fittings are responsible for the warp. The Council Chamber might be a London Board-room. Perhaps after long years among the pens and papers its occupants grow to think that it really is, and in this belief give *résumés* of the history of Local Self-Government in England.

The black frock-coat, emphasizing his points with his spectacle-case, is telling his friends how the parish was first the unit of self-government. He then explains how burgesses were elected, and in tones of deep fervor announces: "Commissioners of Sewers are elected in the same way." Whereunto all this lecture? Is he trying to run a motion through under cover of a cloud of words, essaying the well-known "cuttle-fish trick" of the West?

He abandons England for a while, and *now* we get a glimpse of the cloven hoof in a casual reference to Hindus and Mahomedans. The Hindus will lose nothing by the complete establishment of plurality of votes. They will have the control of their own wards as they used to have. So there is race-feeling, to be explained away, even among these beautiful desks. Scratch the Council, and you come to the old, old trouble. The black frock-coat sits down, and a keen-eyed, black-bearded Englishman rises with one hand in his pocket to explain his views on an alteration of the vote qualification. The idea of an amendment seems to have just struck him. He hints that he will bring it forward later on. He is academical like the others, but not half so good a speaker. All this is dreary beyond words. Why do they talk and talk about owners and occupiers and burgesses in England and the growth of autonomous institutions when the city, the great city, is here crying out to be cleansed? What has England to do with Calcutta's evil, and why should Englishmen be forced to wander through mazes of unprofitable argument against men who cannot understand the iniquity of dirt?

A pause follows the black-bearded man's speech. Rises another native, a heavily-built Babu, in a black gown and a strange head-dress. A snowy white strip of cloth is thrown *jharun*-wise over his shoulders. His voice is high, and not always under control. He begins: "I will try to be as brief as possible." This is ominous. By the way, in Council there seems to be no necessity for a form of address. The orators plunge in *medias res,* and only when they are well launched throw an occasional "Sir" toward Sir Steuart Bayley, who sits with one leg doubled under him and a dry pen in his hand. This speaker is no good. He talks, but he says nothing, and he only knows where he is drifting to. He says: "We must remember that we are legislating for the Metropolis of India, and therefore we should borrow our institutions from large English towns, and not from parochial institutions." If you think for a minute, that shows a large and healthy knowledge of the history of Local Self-Government. It also reveals the attitude of Calcutta. If the city thought less about itself as a metropolis and more as a midden, its state would be better. The speaker talks patronizingly of "my friend," alluding to the black frock-coat. Then he flounders afresh, and his voice gallops up the gamut as he declares, "and therefore that makes all the difference." He hints vaguely at threats, something to do with the Hindus and the Mahomedans, but what he means it is difficult to discover. Here, however, is a sentence taken *verbatim.* It is not likely to appear in this form in the Calcutta papers. The black frock-coat had said that if a wealthy native "had eight votes to his credit, his vanity would prompt him to go to the polling-booth, because he would feel better than half-a-dozen *gharri-wans* or petty traders." (Fancy allowing a *gharri-wan* to vote! He has yet to learn how to drive!) Hereon the gentleman with the white cloth: "Then the complaint is that influential voters will not take the trouble to vote. In my humble opinion, if that be so, adopt voting papers. *That* is the way to meet them. In the same way—The Calcutta Trades' Association—you abolish all plurality of votes: and that is the way to meet *them*." Lucid, is it not? Up flies the irresponsible voice, and delivers this statement: "In the election for the House of Commons plurality are allowed for persons having interest in different districts." Then hopeless, hopeless fog. It is a great pity that India ever heard of anybody higher than the heads of the Civil Service. The country appeals from the *Chota* to the *Burra Sahib* all too readily as it is. Once more a whiff. The gentleman gives a defiant jerk of his shoulder-cloth, and sits down.

Then Sir Steuart Bayley: "The question before the Council is," etc. There is a ripple of "Ayes" and "Noes," and the "Noes" have it, whatever it may be. The black-bearded gentleman springs his amendment about the voting qualifications. A large senator in a white waistcoat, and with a most genial smile, rises and proceeds to smash up the amendment. Can't see the use of it. Calls it in effect rubbish. The black frock-coat rises to explain his friend's amendment, and incidentally makes a funny little slip. He is a knight, and his friend has been newly knighted. He refers to him as "Mister." The black *choga*, he who spoke first of all, speaks again, and talks of the "*sojorner* who comes here for a little time, and then leaves the land." Well it is for the black *choga* that the sojourner does come, or there would be no comfy places wherein to talk about the power that can be measured by wealth and the intellect "which, sir, I submit, cannot be so measured." The amendment is lost, and trebly and quadruply lost is the listener. In the name of sanity and to preserve the tattered shirt tails of a torn illusion, let us escape. This is the Calcutta Municipal Bill. They have been at it for several Saturdays. Last Saturday Sir Steuart Bayley pointed out that at their present rate they would be about two years in getting it through. Now they will sit till dusk, unless Sir Steuart Bayley, who wants to see Lord Connemara off, puts up the black frock-coat to move an adjournment. It is not good to see a Government close to. This leads to the formation of blatantly self-satisfied judgments, which may be quite as wrong as the cramping system with which we have encompassed ourselves. And in the streets outside Englishmen summarize the situation brutally, thus: "The whole thing is a farce. Time is money to us. We can't stick out those everlasting speeches in the municipality. The natives choke us off, but we know that if things get too bad the Government will step in and interfere, and so we worry along somehow." Meantime Calcutta continues to cry out for the bucket and the broom.

CHAPTER IV

ON THE BANKS OF THE HUGLI

THE clocks of the city have struck two. Where can a man get food? Calcutta is not rich in respect of dainty accommodation. You can stay your stomach at Peliti's or Bonsard's, but their shops are not to be found in Hasting Street, or in the places where brokers fly to and fro in office-jauns, sweating and growing visibly *rich*. There must be some sort of entertainment where sailors congregate. "Honest Bombay Jack" supplies nothing but Burma cheroots and whisky in liquor-glasses, but in Lal Bazar, not far from "The Sailors' Coffee-rooms," a board gives bold advertisement that "officers and seamen can find good quarters." In evidence a row of neat officers and seamen are sitting on a bench by the "hotel" door smoking. There is an almost military likeness in their clothes. Perhaps "Honest Bombay Jack" only keeps one kind of felt hat and one brand of suit. When Jack of the mercantile marine is sober, he is very sober. When he is drunk he is—but ask the river police what a lean, mad Yankee can do with his nails and teeth. These gentlemen smoking on the bench are impassive almost as Red Indians. Their attitudes are unrestrained, and they do not wear braces. Nor, it would appear from the bill of fare, are they particular as to what they eat when they attend *tâble d'hôte.* The fare is substantial and the regulation peg—every house has its own depth of peg if you will refrain from stopping Ganymede—something to wonder at. Three fingers and a trifle over seems to be the use of the officers and seamen who are talking so quietly in the doorway. One says—he has evidently finished a long story—"and so he shipped for four pound ten with a first mate s certificate and all, and that was in a German barque." Another spits with conviction and says genially, without raising his voice: "That was a hell of a ship; who knows her?" No answer from the *panchayet,* but a Dane or a German wants to know whether the *Myra* is "up" yet. A dry, red-haired man gives her exact position in the river—(How in the world can he know?)—and the probable hour of her arrival. The grave debate drifts into a discussion of a recent river accident, whereby a big steamer was damaged, and had to put back and discharge cargo. A burly gentleman who is taking a constitutional down Lal Bazar strolls up and says: "I tell you she fouled her own chain with her own forefoot. Hev you seen the plates?" "No." Then how the —— can any —— like you —— say what it—— well was?" He passes on, having delivered his highly-flavored opinion without heat or passion. No one seems to resent the expletives.

Let us get down to the river and see this stamp of men more thoroughly. Clarke Russell has told us that their lives are hard enough in all conscience. What are their pleasures and diversions? The Port Office, where lives the gentlemen who make improvements in the Port of Calcutta, ought to supply information. It stands large and fair, and built in an orientalized manner after the Italians at the corner of Fairlie Place upon the great Strand Road, and a continual clamor of traffic by land and by sea goes up throughout the day and far into the night against its windows. This is a place to enter more reverently than the Bengal Legislative Council, for it houses the direction of the uncertain Hugli down tc the Sandheads, owns enormous wealth, and spends huge sums on the frontaging of river banks, the expansion of jetties, and the manufacture of docks costing two hundred lakhs of rupees. Two million tons of sea-going shippage yearly find their way up and down the river by the guidance of the Port Office, and the men of the Port Office know more than it is good for men to hold in their heads. They can without reference to telegraphic bulletins give the position of all the big steamers, coming up or going down, from the Hugli to the sea, day by day with their tonnage, the names of their captains and the nature of their cargo. Looking out from the veranda of their officer over a lancer-regiment of masts, they can declare truthfully the name of every ship within eye-scope, with the day and hour when she will depart.

In a room at the bottom of the building lounge big men, carefully dressed. Now there is a type of face which belongs almost exclusively to Bengal Cavalry officers—majors for choice. Everybody knows the bronzed, black-moustached, clear-speaking Native Cavalry officer. He exists unnaturally in novels, and naturally on the frontier. These men in the big room have its caste of face so strongly marked that one marvels what officers are doing by the river. "Have they come to book passengers for home?" "Those men! They're pilots. Some of them draw between two and three thousand rupees a month. They are responsible for half-a-million pounds' worth of cargo sometimes." They certainly are men, and they carry themselves as such. They confer together by twos and threes, and appeal frequently to shipping lists.

"*Isn't* a pilot a man who always wears a pea-jacket and shouts through a speaking-trumpet?" "Well, you can ask those gentlemen if you like.

You've got your notions from home pilots. Ours aren't that kind exactly. They are a picked service, as carefully weeded as the Indian Civil. Some of 'em have brothers in it, and some belong to the old Indian army families." But they are not all equally well paid. The Calcutta papers sometimes echo the groans of the junior pilots who are not allowed the handling of ships over a certain tonnage. As it is yearly growing cheaper to build one big steamer than two little ones, these juniors are crowded out, and, while the seniors get their thousands, some of the youngsters make at the end of one month exactly thirty rupees. This is a grievance with them; and it seems well-founded.

In the flats above the pilots' room are hushed and chapel-like offices, all sumptuously fitted, where Englishmen write and telephone and telegraph, and deft Babus forever draw maps of the shifting Hugli. Any hope of understanding the work of the Port Commissioners is thoroughly dashed by being taken through the Port maps of a quarter of a century past. Men have played with the Hugli as children play with a gutter-runnel, and, in return, the Hugli once rose and played with men and ships till the Strand Road was littered with the raffle and the carcasses of big ships. There are photos on the walls of the cyclone of '64, when the *Thunder* came inland

and sat upon an American barque, obstructing all the traffic. Very curious are these photos, and almost impossible to believe. How can a big, strong steamer have her three masts razed to deck level? How can a heavy, country boat be pitched on to the poop of a high-walled liner? and how can the side be bodily torn out of a ship? The photos say that all these things are possible, and men aver that a cyclone may come again and scatter the craft like chaff. Outside the Port Office are the export and import sheds, buildings that can hold a ship's cargo a-piece, all standing on reclaimed ground. Here be several strong smells, a mass of railway lines, and a multitude of men. "Do you see where that trolly is standing, behind the big P. and O. berth? In that place as nearly as may be the *Govindpur* went down about twenty years ago, and began to shift out!" "But that is solid ground." "She sank there, and the next tide made a scour-hole on one side of her. The returning tide knocked her into it. Then the mud made up behind her. Next tide the business was repeated—always the scour-hole in the mud and the filling up behind her. So she rolled and was pushed out and out until she got in the way of the shipping right out yonder, and we had to blow her up. When a ship sinks in mud or quicksand she regularly digs her own grave and wriggles herself into it deeper and deeper till she reaches moderately solid stuff. Then she sticks." Horrible idea, is it not, to go down and down with each tide into the foul Hugli mud?

Close to the Port Offices is the Shipping Office, where the captains engage their crews. The men must produce their discharges from their last ships in the presence of the shipping master, or as they call him—"The Deputy Shipping." He passes them as correct after having satisfied himself that they are not deserters from other ships, and they then sign articles for the voyage. This is the ceremony, beginning with the "dearly beloved" of the crew-hunting captain down to the "amazement" of the identified deserter. There is a dingy building, next door to the Sailors' Home, at whose gate stand the cast-ups of all the seas in all manner of raiment. There are Seedee boys, Bombay *serangs* and Madras fishermen of the salt villages, Malays who insist upon marrying native women grow jealous and run *amok:* Malay-Hindus, Hindu-Malay-whites, Burmese, Burma-whites, Burma-native-whites, Italians with gold earrings and a thirst for gambling, Yankees of all the States, with Mulattoes and pure buck-niggers, red and rough Danes, Cingalese, Cornish boys who seem fresh taken from the plough-tail "corn-stalks from colonial ships where they got four pound ten a month as seamen, tun-bellied Germans, Cockney mates keeping a little aloof from the crowd and talking in knots together, unmistakable "Tommies" who have tumbled into seafaring life by some mistake, cockatoo-tufted Welshmen spitting and swearing like cats, broken-down loafers, grey-headed, penniless, and pitiful, swaggering boys, and very quiet men with gashes and cuts on their faces. It is an ethnological museum where all the specimens are playing comedies and tragedies. The head of it all is the "Deputy Shipping," and he sits, supported by an English policeman whose fists are knobby, in a great Chair of State. The "Deputy Shipping" knows all the iniquity of the riverside, all the ships, all the captains, and a fair amount of the men. He is fenced off from the crowd by a strong wooden railing, behind which are gathered those who "stand and wait," the unemployed of the mercantile marine. They have had their spree—poor devils—and now they will go to sea again on as low a wage as three pound ten a month, to fetch up at the end in some Shanghai stew or San Francisco hell. They have turned their backs on the seductions of the Howrah boarding-houses and the delights of Colootollah. If Fate will, "Nightingales" will know them no more for a season, and their successors may paint Collinga Bazar vermilion. But what captain will take some of these battered, shattered wrecks whose hands shake and whose eyes are red?

Enter suddenly a bearded captain, who has made his selection from the crowd on a previous day, and now wants to get his men passed. He is not fastidious in his choice. His eleven seem a tough lot for such a mild-eyed, civil-spoken man to manage. But the captain in the Shipping Office and the captain on the ship are two different things. He brings his crew up to the "Deputy Shipping's" bar, and hands in their greasy, tattered discharges. But the heart of the "Deputy Shipping" is hot within him, because, two days ago, a Howrah crimp stole a whole crew from a down-dropping ship, insomuch that the captain had to come back and whip up a new crew at one o'clock in the day. Evil will it be if the "Deputy Shipping" finds one of these bounty-jumpers in the chosen crew of the *Blenkindoon,* let us say.

The "Deputy Shipping" tells the story with heat. "I didn't know they did such things in Calcutta," says the captain. "Do such things! They'd steal the eye-teeth out of your head there, Captain." He picks up a discharge and calls for Michael Donelly, who is a loose-knit, vicious-looking Irish-American who chews. "Stand up, man, stand up!" Michael Donelly wants to lean against the desk, and the English policeman won't have it. "What was your last ship?" "*Fairy Queen.*" "When did you leave her?" "'Bout 'leven days." "Captain's name?" "Flahy." "That'll do. Next man: Jules Anderson." Jules Anderson is a Dane. His statements tally with the discharge-certificate of the United States, as the Eagle attesteth. He is passed and falls back. Slivey, the Englishman, and David, a huge plum-colored negro who ships as cook are also passed. Then comes Bassompra, a little Italian, who speaks English. "What's your last ship?" "*Ferdinand.*" "No, after that?" "German barque." Bassompra does not look happy. "When did she sail?" "About three weeks ago." "What's her name?" "*Haidée.*" "You deserted from her?" "Yes, but she's left port." The "Deputy Shipping" runs rapidly through a shipping-list, throws it down with a bang. "'Twon't do. No German barque *Haidée* here for three months. How do I know you don't belong to the *Jackson's* crew? Cap'ain, I'm afraid you'll have to ship another man. He must stand over. Take the rest away and make 'em sign."

The bead-eyed Bassompra seems to have lost his chance of a voyage, and his case will be inquired into. The captain departs with his men and they sign articles for the voyage, while the "Deputy Shipping" tells strange tales of the sailorman's life. "They'll quit a good ship for the sake of a spree, and catch on again at three pound ten, and by Jove, they'll let their skippers pay 'em at ten rupees to the sovereign—poor beggars! As soon as the money's gone they'll ship, but not before. Every one under rank of captain engages here. The competition makes first mates ship sometimes for five pounds or as low as four ten a month." (The gentleman in the boarding-house was right, you see.) "A first mate's wages are seven ten or eight, and foreign captains ship for twelve pounds a month and bring their own small stores—everything, that is to say, except beef, peas, flour, coffee and molasses."

These things are not pleasant to listen to while the hungry-eyed men in the bad clothes lounge and scratch and loaf behind the railing. What comes to them in the end? They die, it seems, though that is not altogether strange. They die at sea in strange and horrible ways; they die, a few of them, in the Kintals, being lost and suffocated in the great sink of Calcutta; they die in strange places by the water-side, and the Hugli takes them away under the mooring chains and the buoys, and casts them up on the sands below, if the River Police have missed the capture. They sail the sea because they must live; and there is no end to their toil. Very, very few find haven of any kind, and the earth, whose ways they do not understand, is cruel to them, when they walk upon it to drink and be merry after the manner of beasts. Jack ashore is a pretty thing when he is in a book or in the blue jacket of the Navy. Mercantile Jack is not so lovely. Later on, we will see where his "sprees" lead him.

CHAPTER V

WITH THE CALCUTTA POLICE

"The City was of Night—perchance of Death,
But certainly of Night."
—*The City of Dreadful Night.*

IN the beginning, the Police were responsible. They said in a patronizing way that, merely as a matter of convenience, they would prefer to take a wanderer round the great city themselves, sooner than let him contract a broken head on his own account in the slums. They said that there were places and places where a white man, unsupported by the arm of the law, would be robbed and mobbed; and that there were other places where drunken seamen would make it very unpleasant for him. There was a night fixed for the patrol, but apologies were offered beforehand for the comparative insignificance of the tour.

"Come up to the fire lookout in the first place, and then you'll be able to see the city." This was at No. 22, Lal Bazar, which is the headquarters of the Calcutta Police, the centre of the great web of telephone wires where Justice sits all day and all night looking after one million people and a floating population of one hundred thousand. But her work shall be dealt with later on. The fire lookout is a little sentry-box on the top of the three-storied police offices. Here a native watchman waits always, ready to give warning to the brigade below if the smoke rises by day or the flames by night in any ward of the city. From this eyrie, in the warm night, one hears the heart of Calcutta beating. Northward, the city stretches away three long miles, with three more miles of suburbs beyond, to Dum-Dum and Barrackpore. The lamplit dusk on this side is full of noises and shouts and smells. Close to the Police Office, jovial mariners at the sailors' coffee-shop are roaring hymns. Southerly, the city's confused lights give place to the orderly lamp-rows of the *maidan* and Chouringhi, where the respectabilities live and the Police have very little to do. From the east goes up to the sky the clamor of Sealdah, the rumble of the trams, and the voices of all Bow Bazar chaffering and making merry. Westward are the business quarters, hushed now, the lamps of the shipping on the river, and the twinkling lights on the Howrah side. It is a wonderful sight—this Pisgah view of a huge city resting after the labors of the day. "Does the noise of traffic go on all through the hot weather?" "Of course. The hot months are the busiest in the year and money's tightest. You should see the brokers cutting about at that season. Calcutta *can't* stop, my dear sir." "What happens then?" "Nothing happens; the death-rate goes up a little. That's all!" Even in February, the weather would, up-country, be called muggy and stifling, but Calcutta is convinced that it is her cold season. The noises of the city grow perceptibly; it is the night side of Calcutta waking up and going abroad. Jack in the sailors' coffee-shop is singing joyously: "Shall we gather at the River—the beautiful, the beautiful, the River?" What an incongruity there is about his selections. However, that it amuses before it shocks the listeners, is not to be doubted. An Englishman, far from his native land is liable to become careless, and it would be remarkable if he did otherwise in ill-smelling Calcutta. There is a clatter of hoofs in the courtyard below. Some of the Mounted Police have come in from somewhere or other out of the great darkness. A clog-dance of iron hoof follows, and an Englishman's voice is heard soothing an agitated horse who seems to be standing on his hind legs. Some of the Mounted Police are going out into the great darkness. "What's on?" "Walk round at Government House. The

Reserve men are being formed up below. They're calling the roll." The Reserve men are all English, and big English at that. They form up and tramp out of the courtyard to line Government Place, and see that Mrs. Lollipop's brougham does not get smashed up by Sirdar Chuckerbutty Bahadur's lumbering C-spring barouche with the two raw Walers. Very military men are the Calcutta European Police in their set-up, and he who knows their composition knows some startling stories of gentlemen-rankers and the like. They are, despite the wearing climate they work in and the wearing work they do, as fine five-score of Englishmen as you shall find east of Suez.

Listen for a moment from the fire lookout to the voices of the night, and you will see why they must be so. Two thousand sailors of fifty nationalities are adrift in Calcutta every Sunday, and of these perhaps two hundred are distinctly the worse for liquor. There is a mild row going on, even now, somewhere at the back of Bow Bazar, which at nightfall fills with sailor-men who have a wonderful gift of falling foul of the native population. To keep the Queen's peace is of course only a small portion of Police duty, but it is trying. The burly president of the lock-up for European drunks—Calcutta central lock-up is worth seeing—rejoices in a sprained thumb just now, and has to do his work left-handed in consequence. But his left hand is a marvelously persuasive one, and when on duty his sleeves are turned up to the shoulder that the jovial mariner may see that there is no deception. The president's labors are handicapped in that the road of sin to the lock-up runs through a grimy little garden—the brick paths are worn deep with the tread of many drunken feet—where a man can give a great deal of trouble by sticking his toes into the ground and getting mixed up with the shrubs. "A straight run in" would be much more convenient both for the president and the drunk. Generally speaking—and here Police experience is pretty much the same all over the civilized world—a woman drunk is a good deal worse than a man drunk. She scratches and bites like a Chinaman and swears like several fiends. Strange people may be unearthed in the lock-ups. Here is a perfectly true story, not three weeks old. A visitor, an unofficial one, wandered into the native side of the spacious accommodation provided for those who have gone or done wrong. A wild-eyed Babu rose from the fixed charpoy and said in the best of English: "Good-morning, sir." "*Good*-morning; who are you, and what are you in for?" Then the Babu, in one breath: "I would have you know that I do not go to prison as a criminal but as a reformer. You've read the *Vicar of Wakefield*"? "Ye-es." "Well, *I* am the Vicar of Bengal—at least that's what I call myself." The visitor collapsed. He had not nerve enough to continue the conversation. Then said the voice of the authority: "He's down in connection with a cheating case at Serampore. May be shamming. But he'll be looked to in time."

The best place to hear about the Police is the fire lookout. From that eyrie one can see how difficult must be the work of control over the great, growling beast of a city. By all means let us abuse the Police, but let us see what the poor wretches have to do with their three thousand natives and one hundred Englishmen. From Howrah and Bally and the other suburbs at least a hundred thousand people come in to Calcutta for the day and leave at night. Also Chandernagore is handy for the fugitive law-breaker, who can enter in the evening and get away before the noon of the next day, having marked his house and broken into it.

"But how can the prevalent offence be housebreaking in a place like this?" "Easily enough. When you've seen a little of the city you'll see. Natives sleep and lie about all over the place, and whole quarters are just so many rabbit-warrens. Wait till you see the Machua Bazar. Well, besides the petty theft and burglary, we have heavy cases of forgery and fraud, that leaves us with our wits pitted against a Bengali's. When a Bengali criminal is working a fraud of the sort he loves, he is *about* the cleverest soul you could wish for. He gives us cases a year long to unravel. Then there are the murders in the low houses—very curious things they are. You'll see the house where Sheikh Babu was murdered presently, and you'll understand. The Burra Bazar and Jora Bagan sections are the two worst ones for heavy cases; but Colootollah is the most aggravating. There's Colootollah over yonder—that patch of darkness beyond the lights. That section is full of tuppenny-ha'penny petty cases, that keep the men up all night and make 'em swear. You'l. see Colootollah, and then perhaps you'll understand. Bamun Bustee is the quietest of all, and Lal Bazar and Bow Bazar, as you can see for yourself, are the rowdiest. You've no notion what the natives come to the *thannahs* for. A *naukar* will come in and want a summons against his master for refusing him half-an-hour's *chuti.* I suppose it *does* seem rather revolutionary to an up-country man, but they try to do it here. Now wait a minute, before we go down into the city and see the Fire Brigade turned out. Business is slack with them just now, but you time 'em and see." An order is given, and a bell strikes softly thrice. There is an orderly rush of men, the click of a bolt, a red fire-engine, spitting and swearing with the sparks flying from the furnace, is dragged out of its shelter. A huge brake, which holds supplementary horses, men, and hatchets, follows, and a hose-cart is the third on the list. The men push the heavy things about as though they were pith toys. Five horses appear. Two are shot into the fire-engine, two—monsters these—into the brake, and the fifth, a powerful beast, warranted to trot fourteen miles an hour, backs into the hose-cart shafts. The men clamber up, some one says softly, "All ready there," and with an angry whistle the fire-engine, followed by the other two, flies out into Lal Bazar, the sparks trailing behind. Time—1 min. 40 secs. "They'll find out it's a false alarm, and come back again in five minutes." "Why?" "Because there will be no constables on the road to give 'em the direction of the fire, and because the driver wasn't told the ward of the outbreak when he went out!" "Do you mean to say that you can from this absurd pigeon-loft locate the wards in the night-time?" "Of course: what would be the good of a lookout if the man couldn't tell where the fire was?" "But it's all pitchy black, and the lights are so confusing."

"Ha! Ha! You'll be more confused in ten minutes. You'll have lost your way as you never lost it before. You're going to go round Bow Bazar section."

"And the Lord have mercy on my soul!" Calcutta, the darker portion of it, does not look an inviting place to dive into at night.

CHAPTER VI

THE CITY OF DREADFUL NIGHT

"And since they cannot spend or use aright
The little time here given them in trust,
But lavish it in weary undelight
Of foolish toil, and trouble, strife and lust—
They naturally claimeth to inherit
The Everlasting Future—that their merit
May have full scope. . . . As surely is most
just." —*The City of Dreadful Night.*

THE difficulty is to prevent this account from growing steadily unwholesome. But one cannot rake through a big city without encountering muck.

The Police kept their word. In five short minutes, as they had prophesied, their charge was lost as he had never been lost before. "Where are we now?" "Somewhere off the Chitpore Road, but you wouldn't understand if you were told. Follow now, and step pretty much where we step—there's a good deal of filth hereabouts."

The thick, greasy night shuts in everything. We have gone beyond the ancestral houses of the Ghoses of the Boses, beyond the lamps, the smells, and the crowd of Chitpore Road, and have come to a great wilderness of packed houses —just such mysterious, conspiring tenements as Dickens would have loved. There is no breath of breeze here, and the air is perceptibly warmer. There is little regularity in the drift, and the utmost niggardliness in the spacing of what, for want of a better name, we must call the streets. If Calcutta keeps such luxuries as Commissioners of Sewers and Paving, they die before they reach this place. The air is heavy with a faint, sour stench—the essence of long-neglected abominations—and it cannot escape from among the tall, three-storied houses. "This, my dear sir, is a *perfectly* respectable quarter as quarters go. That house at the head of the alley, with the elaborate stucco-work round the top of the door, was built long ago by a celebrated midwife. Great people used to live here once. Now it's the—Aha! Look out for that carriage." A big mail-phaeton crashes out of the darkness and, recklessly driven, disappears. The wonder is how is it ever got into this maze of narrow streets, where nobody seems to be moving, and where the dull throbbing of the city's life only comes faintly and by snatches. "Now it's the what?" "St. John's Wood of Calcutta—for the rich Babus. That 'fitton' belonged to one of them." "Well, it's not much of a place to look at?" "Don't judge by appearances. About here live the women who have beggared kings. We aren't going to let you down into unadulterated vice all at once. You must see it first with the gilding on—and mind that rotten board."

Stand at the bottom of a lift and look upward. Then you will get both the size and the design of the tiny courtyard round which one of these big dark houses is built. The central square may be perhaps ten feet every way, but the balconies that run inside it overhang, and seem to cut away half the available space. To reach the square a man must go round many corners, down a covered-in way, and up and down two or three baffling and confused steps. There are no lamps to guide, and the janitors of the establishment seem to be compelled to sleep in the passages. The central square, the *patio* or whatever it must be called, reeks with the faint, sour smell which finds its way impartially into every room. "Now you will understand," say the Police kindly, as their charge blunders, shin-first, into a well-dark winding staircase, "that these are not the sort of places to visit alone." "Who wants to? Of all the disgusting, inaccessible dens—Holy Cupid, what's this?"

A glare of light on the stair-head, a clink of innumerable bangles, a rustle of much fine gauze. and the Dainty Iniquity stands revealed, blazing

—literally blazing—with jewelery from head to foot. Take one of the fairest miniatures that the Delhi painters draw, and multiply it by ten; throw in one of Angelica Kaufmann's best portraits, and add anything that you can think of from Beckford to Lalla Rookh, and you will still fall short of the merits of that perfect face. For an instant, even the grim, professional gravity of the Police is relaxed in the presence of the Dainty Iniquity with the gems, who so prettily invites every one to be seated, and proffers such refreshments as she conceives the palates of the barbarians would prefer. Her Abigails are only one degree less gorgeous than she. Half a lakh, or fifty thousand pounds' worth—it is easier to credit the latter statement than the former—are disposed upon her little body. Each hand carries five jeweled rings which are connected by golden chains to a great jeweled boss of gold in the centre of the back of the hand. Earrings weighted with emeralds and pearls, diamond nose-rings, and how many other hundred articles make up the list of adornments. English furniture of a gorgeous and gimcrack kind, unlimited chandeliers and a collection of atrocious Continental prints—something, but not altogether, like the glazed plaques on *bon-bon* boxes—are scattered about the house, and on every landing —let us trust this is a mistake—lies, squats, or loafs a Bengali who can talk English with unholy fluency. The recurrence suggests—only suggests, mind—a grim possibility of the affectation of excessive virtue by day, tempered with the sort of unwholesome enjoyment after dusk—this loafing and lobbying and chattering and smoking, and unless the bottles lie, tippling among the foul-tongued handmaidens of the Dainty Iniquity. How many men follow this double, deleterious sort of life? The Police are discreetly dumb.

"Now *don't* go talking about 'domiciliary visits' just because this one happens to be a pretty woman. We've *got* to know these creatures. They make the rich man and the poor spend their money; and when a man can't get money for 'em honestly, he comes under *our* notice. *Now* do you see? If there was any domiciliary 'visit' about it, the whole houseful would be hidden past our finding as soon as we turned up in the courtyard. We're friends—to a certain extent." And, indeed, it seemed no difficult thing to be friends to any extent with the Dainty Iniquity who was so surpassingly different from all that experience taught of the beauty of the East. Here was the face from which a man could write *Lalla Rookhs* by the dozen, and believe every work that he wrote. Hers was the beauty that Byron sang of when he wrote—

"Remember, if you come here alone, the chances

are that you'll be clubbed, or stuck, or, anyhow, mobbed. You'll understand that this part of the world is shut to Europeans—absolutely. Mind the steps, and follow on." The vision dies out in the smells and gross darkness of the night, in evil, time-rotten brickwork, and another wilderness of shut-up houses, wherein it seems that people do continually and feebly strum stringed instruments of a plaintive and wailsome nature.

Follows, after another plunge into a passage of a courtyard, and up a staircase, the apparition of a Fat Vice, in whom is no sort of romance, nor beauty, but unlimited coarse humor. She too is studded with jewels, and her house is even finer than the house of the other, and more infested with the extraordinary men who speak such good English and are so deferential to the Police. The Fat Vice has been a great leader of fashion in her day, and stripped a zemindar Raja to his last acre —insomuch that he ended in the House of Correction for a theft committed for her sake. Native opinion has it that she is a "monstrous well-preserved woman." On this point, as on some others, the races will agree to differ.

The scene changes suddenly as a slide in a magic lantern. Dainty Iniquity and Fat Vice slide away on a roll of streets and alleys, each more squalid than its predecessor. We are "somewhere at the back of the Machua Bazar."

well in the heart of the city. There are no houses here—nothing but acres and acres, it seems, of foul wattle-and-dab huts, any one of which would be a disgrace to a frontier village. The whole arrangement is a neatly contrived germ and fire trap, reflecting great credit upon the Calcutta Municipality.

"What happens when these pigsties catch fire?" "They're built up again," say the Police, as though this were the natural order of things. "Land is immensely valuable here." All the more reason, then, to turn several Hausmanns loose into the city, with instructions to make barracks for the population that cannot find room in the huts and sleeps in the open ways, cherishing dogs and worse, much worse, in its unwashen bosom. "Here is a licensed coffee-shop. This is where your *naukers* go for amusement and to see nautches." There is a huge *chappar* shed, ingeniously ornamented with insecure kerosene lamps, and crammed with *gharri-wans, khitmatgars,* small storekeepers and the like. Never a sign of a European. Why? "Because if an Englishman messed about here, he'd get into trouble. Men don't come here unless they're drunk or have lost their way." The *gharri-wans* —they have the privilege of voting, have they not?—look peaceful enough as they squat on tables or crowd by the doors to watch the nautch that is going forward. Five pitiful draggle-tails are huddled together on a bench under one of the lamps, while the sixth is squirming and shrieking before the impassive crowd. She sings of love as understood by the Oriental—the love that dries the heart and consumes the liver. In this place, the words that would look so well on paper, have an evil and ghastly significance. The *gharri-wans* stare or sup tumblers and cups of a filthy decoction, and the *kunchenee* howls with renewed vigor in the presence of the Police. Where the Dainty Iniquity was hung with gold and gems, she is trapped with pewter and glass; and where there was heavy embroidery on the Fat Vice's dress, defaced, stamped tinsel faithfully reduplicates the pattern on the tawdry robes of the *kunchenee*. So you see, if one cares to moralize, they are sisters of the same class.

Two or three men, blessed with uneasy consciences, have quietly slipped out of the coffee-shop into the mazes of the huts beyond. The Police laugh, and those nearest in the crowd laugh applausively, as in duty bound. Perhaps the rabbits grin uneasily when the ferret lands at the bottom of the burrow and begins to clear the warren.

"The *chandoo*-shops shut up at six, so you'll have to see opium-smoking before dark some day. No, you won't, though." The detective nose sniffs, and the detective body makes for a half-opened door of a hut whence floats the fragrance of the black smoke. Those of the inhabitants who are able to stand promptly clear out —they have no love for the Police—and there remain only four men lying down and one standing up. This latter has a pet mongoose coiled round his neck. He speaks English fluently. Yes, he has no fear. It was a private smoking party and— "No business to-night—show how you smoke opium." "Aha! You want to see. Very good, I show. Hiya! you"—he kicks a man on the floor—"show how opium-smoking." The kickee grunts lazily and turns on his elbow. The mongoose, always keeping to the man's neck, erects every hair of its body like an angry cat, and chatters in its owner's ear. The lamp for the opium-pipe is the only one in the room, and lights a scene as wild as anything in the witches' revel; the mongoose acting as the familiar spirit. A voice from the ground says, in tones of infinite weariness: "You take *afim*, so"—a long, long pause, and another kick from the man possessed of the devil—the mongoose. "You take *afim?*" He takes a pellet of the black, treacly stuff on the end of a knitting-needle. "And light *afim.*" He plunges the pellet into the night-light, where it swells and fumes greasily. "And then you put it in your pipe." The smoking pellet is jammed into the tiny bowl of the thick, bamboo-stemmed pipe, and all speech ceases, except the unearthly noise of the mongoose. The man on the ground is sucking at his pipe, and when the smoking pellet has ceased to smoke will be half way to *Nibhan.* "Now you go," says the man with the mongoose. "I am going smoke." The hut door closes upon a red-lit view of huddled legs and bodies, and the man with the mongoose sinking, sinking onto his knees, his head bowed forward, and the little hairy devil chattering on the nape of his neck.

After this the fetid night air seems almost cool, for the hut is as hot as a furnace. "See the *pukka chandu* shops in full blast to-morrow. Now for Colootollah. Come through the huts. There is no decoration about *this* vice."

The huts now gave place to houses very tall and spacious and very dark. But for the narrowness of the streets we might have stumbled upon Chouringhi in the dark. An hour and a half has passed, and up to this time we have not crossed our trail once. "You might knock about the city for a night and never cross the same line. Recollect Calcutta isn't one of your poky up-country cities of a lakh and a half of people." "How long does it take to know it then?" "About a lifetime, and even then some of the streets puzzle you." "How much has the head of a ward to know?" "Every house in his ward if he can, who owns it, what sort of character the inhabitants are, who are their friends, who go out and in, who loaf about the place at night, and so on and so on." "And he knows all this by night as well as by day?" "Of course. Why shouldn't he?" "No reason in the world. Only it's pitchy black just now, and I'd like to see where this alley is going to end." "Round the corner beyond that dead wall. There's a lamp there. Then you'll be able to see." A shadow flits out of a gully and disappears. "Who's that?" "Sergeant of Police just to see where we're going in case of accidents." Another shadow staggers into the darkness. "Who's *that?*" "Man from the fort or a sailor from the ships. I couldn't quite see." The Police open a shut door in a high wall, and stumble unceremoniously among a gang of women cooking their food. The floor is of beaten earth, the steps that lead into the upper stories are unspeakably grimy, and the heat is the heat of April. The women rise hastily, and the light of the bull's eye—for the Police have now lighted a lantern in regular "rounds of London" fashion—shows six bleared faces—one a half native half Chinese one, and the others Bengali. "There are no men here!" they cry.

"The house is empty." Then they grin and jabber and chew *pan* and spit, and hurry up the steps into the darkness. A range of three big rooms has been knocked into one here, and there is some sort of arrangement of mats. But an average country-bred is more sumptuously accommodated in an Englishman's stable. A home horse would snort at the accommodation.

"Nice sort of place, isn't it?" say the Police, genially. "This is where the sailors get robbed and drunk." "They must be blind drunk before they come." "Na—Na! Na sailor men ee—yah!" chorus the women, catching at the one word they understand. "Arl gone!" The Police take no notice, but tramp down the big room with the mat loose-boxes. A woman is shivering in one of these. "What's the matter?" "Fever. Seek. Vary, *vary* seek." She huddles herself into a heap on the *charpoy* and groans.

A tiny, pitch-black closet opens out of the long room, and into this the Police plunge. "Hullo! What's here?" Down flashes the lantern, and a white hand with black nails comes out of the gloom. Somebody is asleep or drunk in the cot. The ring of lantern light travels slowly up and down the body. "A sailor from the ships. He's got his *dungarees* on. He'll be robbed before the morning most likely." The man is sleeping like a little child, both arms thrown over his head, and he is not unhandsome. He is shoeless, and there are huge holes in his stockings. He is a pure-blooded white, and carries the flush of innocent sleep on his cheeks.

The light is turned off, and the Police depart; while the woman in the loose-box shivers, and moans that she is "seek: vary, *vary* seek." It is not surprising.

CHAPTER VII

DEEPER AND DEEPER STILL

I built myself a lordly pleasure-house,
  Wherein at ease for aye to dwell;
I said: "O Soul, make merry and carouse.
  Dear Soul—for all is well."

—*The Palace of Art.*

"AND where next? I don't like Colootollah." The Police and their charge are standing in the interminable waste of houses under the starlight. "To the lowest sink of all," say the Police after the manner of Virgil when he took the Italian with the indigestion to look at the frozen sinners. "And where's that?" "Somewhere about here; but you wouldn't know if you were told." They lead and they lead and they lead, and they cease not from leading till they come to the last circle of the Inferno—a long, long, winding, quiet road. "There you are; you can see for yourself."

But there is nothing to be seen. On one side are houses—gaunt and dark, naked and devoid of furniture; on the other, low, mean stalls, lighted, and with shamelessly open doors, wherein women stand and lounge, and mutter and whisper one to another. There is a hush here, or at least the busy silence of an officer of counting-house in working hours. One look down the street is sufficient. Lead on, gentlemen of the Calcutta Police. Let us escape from the lines of open doors, the flaring lamps within, the glimpses of the tawdry toilet-tables adorned with little plaster dogs, glass balls from Christmas-trees, and—for religion must not be despised though women be fallen—pictures of the saints and statuettes of the Virgin. The street is a long one, and other streets, full of the same pitiful wares, branch off from it.

"Why are they so quiet? Why don't they make a row and sing and shout, and so on?" "Why should they, poor devils?" say the Police, and fall to telling tales of horror, of women decoyed into *palkis* and shot into this trap. Then other tales that shatter one's belief in all things and folk of good repute. "How can you Police have faith in humanity?"

"That's because you're seeing it all in a lump for the first time, and it's not nice that way. Makes a man jump rather, doesn't it? But, recollect, you've *asked* for the worst places, and you can't complain." "Who's complaining? Bring on your atrocities. Isn't that a European woman at that door?" "Yes. Mrs. D——.

widow of a soldier, mother of seven children." "Nine, if you please, and good-evening to you," shrills Mrs. D——, leaning against the door-post, her arms folded on her bosom. She is a rather pretty, slightly-made Eurasian, and whatever shame she mav have owned she has long since cast behind her. A shapeless Burmo-native trot, with high cheek-bones and mouth like a shark, calls Mrs. D—— "Mem-Sahib." The word jars unspeakably. Her life is a matter between herself and her Maker, but in that she—the widow of a soldier of the Queen—has stooped to this common foulness in the face of the city, she has offended against the white race. The Police fail to fall in with this righteous indignation. More. They laugh at it out of the wealth of their unholy knowledge. "You're from up-country, and of course you don't understand. There are any amount of that lot in the city." Then the secret of the insolence of Calcutta is made plain. Small wonder the natives fail to respect the Sahib, seeing what they see and knowing what they know. In the good old days, the honorable the directors deported him or her who misbehaved grossly, and the white man preserved his *izzat*. He may have been a ruffian, but he was a ruffian on a large scale. He did not sink in the presence of the people. The natives are quite right to take the wall of the Sahib who has been at great pains to prove that he is of the same flesh and blood.

All this time Mrs. D—— stands on the threshold of her room and looks upon the men with unabashed eyes. If the spirit of that English soldier, who married her long ago by the forms of the English Church, be now flitting bat-wise above the roofs, how singularly pleased and proud it must be! Mrs. D—— is a lady with a story. She is not averse to telling it. "What was—ahem—the case in which you were —er—hmn—concerned, Mrs. D——?" "They said I'd poisoned my husband by putting something into his drinking water." This is interesting. How much modesty *has* this creature? Let us see. "And—ah—*did* you?" "'Twasn't proved," says Mrs. D—— with a laugh, a pleasant, lady-like laugh that does infinite credit to her education and upbringing. Worthy Mrs. D——! It would pay a novelist—a French one let us say—to pick you out of the stews and make you talk.

The Police move forward, into a region of Mrs. D——'s. This is horrible; but they are used to it, and evidently consider indignation affectation. Everywhere are the empty houses, and the babbling women in print gowns. The clocks in the city are close upon midnight, but the Police show no signs of stopping. They plunge hither and thither, like wreckers into the surf; and each plunge brings up a sample of misery, filth and woe.

"Sheikh Babu was murdered just here," they say, pulling up in one of the most troublesome houses in the ward. It would never do to appear ignorant of the murder of Sheikh Babu. "I only wonder that more aren't killed." The houses with their breakneck staircases, their hundred corners, low roofs, hidden courtyards and winding passages, seem specially built for crime of every kind. A woman—Eurasian—rises to a sitting position on a board-charpoy and blinks sleepily at the Police. Then she throws herself down with a grunt. "What's the matter with you?" "I live in Markiss Lane and"—this with intense gravity—"I'm *so* drunk." She has a rather striking gipsy-like face, but her language might be improved.

"Come along," say the Police, "we'll head back to Bentinck Street, and put you on the road to the Great Eastern." They walk long and steadily, and the talk falls on gambling hell. "You ought to see our men rush one of 'em. They like the work—natives of course. When we've marked a hell down, we post men at the entrances and carry it. Sometimes the Chinese bite, but as a rule they fight fair. It's a pity we hadn't a hell to show you. Let's go in here—

there may be something forward." "Here" appears to be in the heart of a Chinese quarter, for the pigtails—do they ever go to bed?—are scuttling about the streets. "Never go into a Chinese place alone," say the Police, and swung open a postern gate in a strong, green door. Two Chinamen appear.

"What are we going to see?" "Japanese gir— No, we aren't, by Jove! Catch that Chinaman, *quick*." The pigtail is trying to double back across a courtyard into an inner chamber; but a large hand on his shoulder spins him round and puts him in rear of the line of advancing Englishmen, who are, be it observed, making a fair amount of noise with their boots. A second door is thrown open, and the visitors advance into a large, square room blazing with gas. Here thirteen pigtails, deaf and blind to the outer world, are bending over a table. The captured Chinaman dodges uneasily in the rear of the procession. Five—ten—fifteen seconds pass, the Englishmen standing in the full light less than three paces from the absorbed gang who see nothing. Then burly Superintendent Lamb brings down his hand on his thigh with a crack like a pistol-shot and shouts: "How do, John?" Follows a frantic rush of scared Celestials, almost tumbling over each other in their anxiety to get clear. Gudgeon before the rush of the pike are nothing to John Chinaman detected in the act of gambling. One pigtail scoops up a pile of copper money, another a chinaware soup-bowl and only a little mound of accusing cowries remains on the white matting that covers the table. In less than half a minute two facts are forcibly brought home to the visitor. First, that a pigtail is largely composed of silk, and rasps the palm of the hand as it slides through; and secondly, that the forearm of a Chinaman is surprisingly muscular and well-developed. "What's going to be done?" "Nothing. They're only three of us, and all the ringleaders would get away. Look at the doors. We've got 'em safe any time we want to catch 'em, if this little visit doesn't make 'em shift their quarters. Hi! John. No pidgin to-night. Show how you makee play. That fat youngster there is our informer."

Half the pigtails have fled into the darkness, but the remainder, assured and trebly assured that the Police really mean "no pidgin," return to the table and stand round while the croupier proceeds to manipulate the cowries, the little curved slip of bamboo and the soup-bowl. They never gamble, these innocents. They only come to look on, and smoke opium in the next room. Yet as the game progresses their eyes light up, and one by one they lose in to deposit their price on odd or even—the number of the cowries that are covered and left uncovered by the little soup-bowl. *Mythan* is the name of the amusement, and, whatever may be its demerits, it is *clean.* The Police look on while their charge plays and oots a parchment-skinned horror—one of Swift's Struldburgs, strayed from Laputa—of the enormous sum of two annas. The return of this wealth, doubled, sets the loser beating his forehead against the table from sheer gratitude.

"*Most* immortal game this. A man might drop five whole rupees, if he began playing at sun-down and kept it up all night. Don't *you* ever play whist occasionally?"

"Now, we didn't bring you round to make fun of this department. A man can lose as much as ever he likes and he can fight as well, and if he loses all his money he steals to get more. A Chinaman is insane about gambling, and half his crime comes from it. It *must* be kept down." "And the other business. Any sort of supervision there?" "No; so long as they keep outside the penal code. Ask Dr. —— about that. It's outside our department. Here we are in Bentinck Street and you can be driven to the Great Eastern in a few minutes. Joss houses? Oh, yes. If you want more horrors, Superintendent Lamb will take you round with him to-morrow afternoon at five. Report yourself at the Bow Bazar Thanna at five minutes to. Good-night."

The Police depart, and in a few minutes the silent, well-ordered respectability of Old Council House Street, with the grim Free Kirk at the end of it, is reached. All good Calcutta has gone to bed, the last tram has passed, and the peace of the night is upon the world. Would it be wise and rational to climb the spire of that kirk, and shout after the fashion of the great Lion-slayer of Tarescon: "O true believers! Decency is a fraud and a sham. There is nothing clean or pure or wholesome under the stars, and we are all going to perdition together. Amen!" On second thoughts it would not; for the spire is slippery, the night is hot, and the Police have been specially careful to warn their charge that he must not be carried away by the sight of horrors that cannot be written or hinted at.

"Good-morning," says the Policeman, tramping the pavement in front of the Great Eastern, and he nods his head pleasantly to show that he is the representative of Law and Peace and that the city of Calcutta is safe from itself for the present.

CHAPTER VIII

CONCERNING LUCIA

"Was a woman such a woman—cheeks so round and lips so red?
On the neck the small head buoyant like the bell flower in its bed."

TIME must be filled in somehow till five this afternoon, when Superintendent Lamb will reveal more horrors. Why not, the trams aiding, go to the Old Park Street Cemetery? It is presumption, of course, because none other than the great Sir W. W. Hunter once went there, and wove from his visit certain fascinating articles for the *Englishman;* the memory of which lingers even to this day, though they were written fully two years since.

But the Great Sir W. W. went in his Legislative Consular brougham and never in an unbridled tram-car which pulled up somewhere in the middle of Dhurrumtollah. "You want go Park Street? No trams going Park Street. You get out here." Calcutta tram conductors are not polite. Some day one of them will be hurt. The car shuffles unsympathetically down the street, and the evicted is stranded in Dhurrumtollah, which may be the Hammersmith Highway of Calcutta. Providence arranged this mistake, and paved the way to a Great Discovery now published for the first time. Dhurrumtollah is full of the People of India, walking in family parties and groups and confidential couples. And the people of India are neither Hindu nor Mussulman—Jew, Ethiop, Gueber nor expatriated British. They are the Eurasians, and there are hundreds and hundreds of them in Dhurrumtollah now. There is Papa with a shining black hat fit for a counsellor of the Queen, and Mamma, whose silken attire is tight upon her portly figure, and The Brood made up of straw-hatted, olive-cheeked, sharp-eyed little boys, and leggy maidens wearing white, open-work stockings calculated to show dust. There are the young men who smoke bad cigars and carry themselves lordily—such as have incomes. There are also the young women with the beautiful eyes and the wonderful dresses which always fit so badly across the shoulders. And they carry prayer-books or baskets, because they are either going to mass or the market. Without doubt, these are the people of India. They were born in it, bred in it, and will die in it. The Englishman only comes to the country, and the natives of course were there from the first, but these people have been made here, and no one has done anything for them except talk and write about them. Yet they belong, some of them, to old and honorable families, hold "houses, messuages, and tenements" in Sealdah, and are rich, a few of them. They all look prosperous and contented, and they chatter eternally in that curious dialect that no one has yet reduced to print. Beyond what little they please to reveal now and again in the newspapers, we know nothing about their life which touches so intimately the white on the one hand and the black on the other. It must be interesting—more interesting than the colorless Anglo-Indian article; but who has treated of it? There was one novel once in which the second heroine was an Eurasienne. She was a strictly subordinate character, and came to a sad end. The poet of the race, Henry Derozio—he of whom Mr. Thomas Edwards wrote a history—was bitten with Keats and Scott and Shelley, and overlooked in his search for material things that lay nearest to him. All this mass of humanity in Dhurrumtollah is unexploited and almost unknown. Wanted, therefore, a writer from among the Eurasians, who shall write so that men shall be pleased to read a story of Eurasian life; then outsiders will be interested in the People of India, and will admit that the race has possibilities.

A futile attempt to get to Park Street from Dhurrumtollah ends in the market—the Hogg

Market men call it. Perhaps a knight of that name built it. It is not one-half as pretty as the Crawford Market, in Bombay but . . . it appears to be the trysting-place of Young Calcutta. The natural inclination of youth is to lie abed late, and to let the seniors do all the hard work. Why, therefore, should Pyramus who has to be ruling account forms at ten, and Thisbe, who *cannot* be interested in the price of second quality beef, wander, in studiously correct raiment, round and about the stalls before the sun is well clear of the earth? Pyramus carries a walking stick with imitation silver straps upon it, and there are cloth tops to his boots; but his collar has been two days worn. Thisbe crowns her dark head with a blue velvet Tam-o'-Shanter; but one of her boots lacks a button, and there is a tear in the left-hand glove. Mamma, who despises gloves, is rapidly filling a shallow basket, that the coolie-boy carries, with vegetables, potatoes, purple brinjals, and—Oh, Pryamus! Do you ever kiss Thisbe when Mamma is not near? —garlic—yea, *lusson* of the bazar. Mamma is generous in her views on garlic. Pryamus comes round the corner of the stall looking for nobody in particular—not he—and is elaborately polite to Mamma. Somehow, he and Thisbe drift off together, and Mamma, very portly and very voluble, is left to chaffer and sort and select alone.

In the name of the Sacred Unities do not, young people, retire to the meat-stalls to exchange confidences! Come up to this end, where the roses are arriving in great flat baskets, where the air is heavy with the fragrance of flowers, and the young buds and greenery are littering all the floor. They won't—they prefer talking by the dead, unromantic muttons, where there are not so many buyers. How they babble! There must have been a quarrel to make up. Thisbe shakes the blue velvet Tam-o'-Shanter and says: "O yess!" scornfully. Pyramus answers: "No-a, no-a. Do-ant say thatt." Mamma's basket is full and she picks up Thisbe hastily. Pyramus departs. *He* never came here to do any marketing. He came to meet Thisbe, who in ten years will own a figure very much like Mamma's. May their ways be smooth before them, and after honest service of the Government, may Pyramus retire on Rs. 250 per mensen, into a nice little house somewhere in Monghyr or Chunar.

From love by natural sequence to death. Where *is* the Park Street Cemetery? A hundred *gharriwans* leap from their boxes and invade the market, and after a short struggle one of them uncarts his capture in a burial-ground—a ghastly new place, close to a tramway. This is not what is wanted. The living dead are here—the people whose names are not yet altogether perished and whose tombstones are tended. "Where are the *old* dead?" "Nobody goes there," says the *gharri-wan*. "It is up that road." He points up a long and utterly deserted thoroughfare, running between high walls. This is the place, and the entrance to it, with its *mallee* waiting with one brown, battered rose, its grilled door and its professional notices, bears a hideous likeness to the entrance of Simla churchyard. But, once inside, the sightseer stands in the heart of utter desolation—all the more forlorn for being swept up. Lower Park Street cuts a great graveyard in two. The guide-books will tell you when the place was opened and when it was closed. The eye is ready to swear that it is as old as Herculaneum and Pompeii. The tombs are small houses. It is as though we walked down the streets of a town, so tall are they and so closely do they stand—a town shriveled by fire, and scarred by frost and siege. They must have been afraid of their friends rising up before the due time that they weighted them with such cruel mounds of masonry. Strong man, weak woman, or somebody's "infant son aged fifteen months"—it is all the same. For each the squat obelisk, the defaced classic temple, the cellaret of chunam, or the candlestick of brickwork—the heavy slab, the rust-eaten railings, the whopper-jawed cherubs and the apoplectic angels. Men were rich in those days and could afford to put a hundred cubic feet of masonry into the grave of even so humble a person as "Jno. Clements, Captain of the Country Service, 1820." When the "dearly beloved" had held rank answering to that of Commissioner, the efforts are still more sumptuous and the verse . . . Well, the following speaks for itself:

> "Soft on thy tomb shall fond Remembrance shed
> The warm yet unavailing tear,
> And purple flowers that deck the honored dead
> Shall strew the loved and honored bier."

Failure to comply with the contract does not, let us hope, entail to forfeiture of the earnest-money; or the honored dead might be grieved. The slab is out of his tomb, and leans foolishly against it; the railings are rotted, and there are no more lasting ornaments than blisters and stains, which are the work of the weather, and not the result of the "warm yet unavailing tear." The eyes that promised to shed them have been closed any time these seventy years.

Let us go about and moralize cheaply on the tombstones, trailing the robe of pious reflection up and down the pathways of the grave. Here is a big and stately tomb sacred to "Lucia," who died in 1776 A. D., aged 23. Here also be verses which an irreverent thumb can bring to light. Thus they wrote, when their hearts were heavy in them, one hundred and sixteen years ago :

"What needs the emblem, what the plaintive strain,
What all the arts that sculpture e'er expressed,
To tell the treasure that these walls contain?
Let those declare it most who knew her best.

"The tender pity she would oft display
Shall be with interest at her shrine returned,
Connubial love, connubial tears repay,
And Lucia loved shall still be Lucia mourned.

"Though closed the lips, though stopped the tuneful breath,
The silent, clay-cold monitress shall teach—
In all the alarming eloquence of death
With double pathos to the heart shall preach.

"Shall teach the virtuous maid, the faithful wife,
If young and fair, that young and fair was she,
Then close the useful lesson of her life,
And tell them what she is, they soon must be."

That goes well, even after all these years, does it not? and seems to bring Lucia very near, in spite of what the later generation is pleased to call the stiltedness of the old-time verse.

Who will declare the merits of Lucia—dead in her spring before there was even a *Hickey's Gazette* to chronicle the amusements of Calcutta, and publish, with scurrilous asterisks, the *liaisons* of heads of departments? What pot-bellied East

Indiaman brought the "virtuous maid" up the river, and did Lucia "make her bargain," as the cant of those times went, on the first, second, or third day after her arrival? Or did she, with the others of the batch, give a spinsters' ball as a last trial—following the custom of the country? No. She was a fair Kentish maiden, sent out, at a cost of five hundred pounds, English money, under the captain's charge, to wed the man of her choice, and *he* knew Clive well, had had dealings with Omichand, and talked to men who had lived through the terrible night in the Black Hole. He was a rich man, Lucia's battered tomb proves it, and he gave Lucia all that her heart could wish. A green-painted boat to take the air in on the river of evenings. Coffree slave-boys who could play on the French horn, and even a very elegant, neat coach with a genteel rutlan roof ornamented with flowers very highly finished, ten best polished plate glasses, ornamented with a few elegant medallions enriched with mother-o'-pearl, that she might take her drive on the course as befitted a factor's wife. All these things he gave her. And when the convoys came up the river, and the guns thundered, and the servants of the Honorable the East India Company drank to the king's health, be sure that Lucia before all the other ladies in the fort had her choice of the new stuffs from England and was cordially hated in consequence. Tilly Kettle painted her picture a little before she died, and the hot-blooded young writers did duel with small swords in the fort ditch for the honor of piloting her through a minuet at the Calcutta theatre or the Punch House. But Warren Hastings danced with her instead, and the writers were confounded—every man of them. She was a toast far up the river. And she walked in the evening on the bastions of Fort-William, and said: "La! I protest!" It was there that she exchanged congratulations with all her friends on the 20th of October, when those who were alive gathered together to felicitate themselves on having come through another hot season; and the men—even the sober factor saw no wrong here—got most royally and Britishly drunk on Madeira that had twice rounded the Cape. But Lucia fell sick, and the doctor—he who went home after seven years with five lakhs and a half, and a corner of this vast graveyard to his account—said that it was a pukka or putrid fever, and the system required strengthening. So they fed Lucia on hot curries, and mulled wine worked up with spirits and fortified with spices, for nearly a week; at the end of which time she closed her eyes on the weary, weary river and the fort forever, and a gallant, with a turn for *belles lettres*, wept openly as men did then and had no shame of it, and composed the verses above set, and thought himself a neat hand at the pen—stap his vitals! But the factor was so grieved that he could write nothing at all—could only spend his money—and he counted his wealth by lakhs—on a sumptuous grave. A little later on he took comfort, and when the next batch came out—

But this has nothing whatever to do with the story of Lucia, the virtuous maid, the faithful wife. Her ghost went to Mrs. Westland's powder ball, and looked very beautiful.

PART SECOND

CHAPTER I

A RAILWAY SETTLEMENT

JAMALPUR is the headquarters of the E. I. Railway. This in itself is not a startling statement. The wonder begins with the exploration of Jamalpur, which is a station entirely made by, and devoted to, the use of those untiring servants of the public, the railway folk. They have towns of their own at Toondla and Assensole, a sun-dried sanitarium at Bandikui; and Howrah, Ajmir, Allahabad, Lahore and Pindi know their colonies. But Jamalpur is unadulteratedly "Railway," and he who has nothing to do with the E. I. Railway in some shape or another feels a stranger and an "interloper." Running always east and southerly, the train carries him from the torments of the northwest into the wet, woolly warmth of Bengal, where may be found the hothouse heat that has ruined the temper of the good people of Calcutta. Here the land is fat and greasy with good living, and the wealth of the bodies of innumerable dead things; and here—just above Mokameh—may be seen fields stretching, without stick, stone or bush to break the view, from the railway line to the horizon.

Up-country innocents must look at the map to

learn that Jamalpur is near the top left-hand corner of the big loop that the E. I. R. throws out round Bhagalpur and part of the Bara-Banki districts. Northward of Jamalpur, as near as may be, lies the Ganges and Tirhoot, and eastward an offshoot of the volcanic Rajmehal range blocks the view.

A station which has neither Judge, Commissioner, Deputy or 'Stunt, which is devoid of law courts, ticca-gharries, District Superintendents of Police, and many other evidences of an overcultured civilization, is a curiosity. "We administer ourselves," says Jamalpur, proudly, "or we did—till we had lokil sluff brought in—and now the racket-marker administers us." This is a solemn fact. The station, which had its beginnings thirty odd years ago, used, till comparatively recent times, to control its own roads, sewage, conservancy, and the like. But, with the introduction of local self-government, it was ordained that the "inestimable boon" should be extended to a place made by, and maintained for, Europeans, and a brand new municipality was created and nominated according to the many rules of the game. In the skirmish that ensued, the club racket-marker fought his way to the front, secured a place on a board largely composed of Babus, and since that day Jamalpur's views on "local sluff" have not been fit for publication. To understand the magnitude of the insult, one must study the city—for station, in the strict sense of the word, it is not. Crotons, palms, mangoes, *mellingtonias*, teak, and bamboos adorn it, and the *ponisettia* and *bougainvillea*, the railway creeper and the *bignonia-venusta* make it gay with many colors. It is laid out with military precision on the right-hand side of the line going down to Calcutta—to each house its just share of garden and green *jilmil*, its red *surki* path, its growth of trees, and its neat little wicket gate. Its general aspect, in spite of the Dutch formality, is that of an English village, such a thing as enterprising stage-managers put on the theatres at home. The hills have thrown a protecting arm round nearly three sides of it, and on the fourth it is bounded by what are locally known as the "shed;" in other words, the station, offices, and workshops of the company. The E. I. R. only exists for outsiders. Its servants speak of it reverently, angrily, despitefully, or enthusiastically as "The Company;" and they never omit the big, big C. Men must have treated the Honorable East India Company in something the same fashion ages ago. "The Company" in Jamalpur is Lord Dufferin, all the Members of Council, the Body-Guard, Sir Frederick Roberts, Mr. Westland, whose name is at the bottom of the currency notes, the

Oriental Life Assurance Company, and the Bengal Government all rolled into one. At first, when a stranger enters this life, he is inclined to scoff and ask, in his ignorance: "*What* is this Company that you talk so much about?" Later on, he ceases to scoff, and his mouth opens slowly; for the Company is a "big" thing—almost big enough to satisfy an American.

Ere beginning to describe its doings, let it be written, and repeated several times hereafter, that the E. I. R. passenger carriages, and especially the second-class, are just now—horrid, being filthy and unwashen, dirty to look at, and dirty to live in. Having cast this small stone, we will examine Jamalpur. When it was laid out, in or before the Mutiny year, its designers allowed room for growth, and made the houses of one general design—some of brick, some of stone, some three, four, and six-roomed, some single men's barracks and some two-storied—all for the use of the *employees.* King's Road, Prince's Road, Queen's Road, and Victoria Road—Jamalpur is loyal—cut the breadth of the station; and Albert Road, Church Street, and Steam Road the length of it. Neither on these roads or on any of the cool-shaded smaller ones is anything unclean or unsightly to be found. There is a dreary *bustee* in the neighborhood which is said to make the most of any cholera that may be going, but

Jamalpur itself is specklessly and spotlessly neat. From St. Mary's Church to the railway station, and from the buildings where they print daily about half a lakh of tickets to the ringing, roaring, rattling workshops, everything has the air of having been cleaned up at ten that very morning and put under a glass case. Also there is a holy calm about the roads—totally unlike anything in an English manufacturing town. Wheeled conveyances are few, because every man's bungalow is close to his work, and when the day has begun and the offices of the "Loco." and "Traffic" have soaked up their thousands of natives and hundreds of Europeans, you shall pass under the dappled shadows of the teak trees, hearing nothing louder than the croon of some bearer playing with a child in the veranda or the faint tinkle of a piano. This is pleasant, and produces an impression of Watteau-like refinement tempered with Arcadian simplicity. The dry, anguished howl of the "buzzer," the big steam-whistle, breaks the hush, and all Jamalpur is alive with the tramping of tiffin-seeking feet. The Company gives one hour for meals between eleven and twelve. On the stroke of noon there is another rush back to the works or the offices, and Jamalpur sleeps through the afternoon till four or half-past, and then rouses for tennis at the institute.

It is a quiet, restful place to live or die in, but not great for enterprise. Tropical or semi-tropical cities are never remarkable for excessive energy or activity. Nor do the inhabitants arrive at fortune made by the exertion of the persons possessing it. Fortunes are made in such places, but by the dull continuous labor of inferiors and natives for some supervisor or director usually foreign.

In the hot weather it splashes in the swimming bath, or reads, for it has a library of several thousand books. One of the most flourishing lodges in the Bengal jurisdiction—"St. George in the East"—lives at Jamalpur, and meets twice a month. Its members point out with justifiable pride that all the fittings were made by their own hands; and the lodge in its accoutrements and the energy of the craftsmen can compare with any in India. But the institute seems to be the central gathering place, and its half-dozen tennis-courts and neatly-laid-out grounds seem to be always full. Here, if a stranger could judge, the greater part of the flirtation of Jamalpur is carried out, and here the dashing apprentice—the apprentices are the liveliest of all—learns that there are problems harder than any he studies at the night school, and that the heart of a maiden is more inscrutable than the mechanism of a locomotive. On Tuesdays and Fridays, as a printed notification witnesseth, the volunteers parade. A and B Companies, one hundred and fifty strong in all, of the E. I. R. Volunteers, are stationed here with the band. Their uniform, grey with red facings, is not lovely, but they know how to shoot and drill. They have to. The "Company" makes it a condition of service that a man must be a volunteer; and volunteer in something more than name he must be, or some one will ask the reason why. Seeing that there are no regulars between Howrah and Dinapore, the "Company" does well in exacting this toll. Some of the old soldiers are wearied of drill, some of the youngsters don't like it, but—the way they entrain and detrain is worth seeing. They are as mobile a corps as can be desired, and perhaps ten or twelve years hence the Government may possibly be led to take a real interest in them and spend a few thousand rupees in providing them with real soldiers' kits—not uniform and rifle merely. Their ranks include all sorts and conditions of men—heads of the "loco." and "traffic," the "Company" is no great respecter of rank—clerks in the "audit," boys from mercantile firms at home, fighting with the intricacies of time, fare and freight tables; guards who have grown grey in the service of the Company; mail and passenger drivers with nerves of cast iron, who can shoot through a long afternoon without losing temper or flurrying; light-built East Indians; Tyne-side men, slow of speech and uncommonly strong in the arm; lathy apprentices who have not yet "filled out;" fitters, turners, foremen, full assistant and sub-assistant station-masters, and a host of others. In the hands of the younger men the regulation Martini-Henri naturally goes off the line occasionally on a *shikar* expedition.

There is a twelve-hundred yards' range running down one side of the station, and the condition of the grass by the firing butts tells its own tale. Scattered in the ranks of the volunteers are a fair number of old soldiers, for the Company has a weakness for recruiting from the army for its guards who may, in time, become station-masters. A good man from the army, with his papers all correct and certificates from his commanding officer, may, after depositing twenty pounds to pay his home passage, in the event of his services being dispensed with, enter the Company's service on something less than one hundred rupees a month and rise in time to four hundred as a station-master. A railway bungalow—and they are as substantially built as the engines—cannot cost him more than one-ninth of the pay of his grade, and the Provident Fund provides for his latter end.

Think for a moment of the number of men that

a line running from Howrah to Delhi must use, and you will realize what an enormous amount of patronage the Company holds in its hands. Naturally a father who has worked for the line expects the line to do something for the son; and the line is not backward in meeting his wishes where possible. The sons of old servants may be taken on at fifteen years of age, or thereabouts, as apprentices in the "shops," receiving twenty rupees in the first and fifty in the last year of the indentures. Then they come on the books as full "men" on perhaps Rs. 65 a month, and the road is open to them in many ways. They may become foremen of departments on Rs. 500 a month, or drivers earning with overtime Rs. 370; or if they have been brought into the audit or the traffic, they may control innumerable Babus and draw several hundreds of rupees monthly; or, at eighteen or nineteen, they may be ticket-collectors, working up to the grade of guard, etc. Every rank of the huge, human hive has a desire to see its sons placed properly, and the native workmen, about three thousand, in the locomotive department only, are, said one man, "making a family affair of it altogether. You see all those men turning brass and looking after the machinery? They've all got relatives, and a lot of 'em own land out Monghyr-way close to us. They bring on their sons as soon as they are old enough to do anything, and the Company rather encourages it. You see the father is in a way responsible for his son, and he'll teach him all he knows, and in that way the Company has a hold on them all. You've no notion how sharp a native is when he's working on his own hook. All the district round here, right up to Monghyr, is more or less dependent on the railway."

The Babus in the traffic department, in the stores, issue department, in all the departments where men sit through the long, long Indian day among ledgers, and check and pencil and deal in figures and items and rupees, may be counted by hundreds. Imagine the struggle among them to locate their sons in comfortable cane-bottomed chairs, in front of a big pewter inkstand and stacks of paper! The Babus make beautiful accountants, and if we could only see it, a merciful Providence has made the Babu for figures and detail. Without him on the Bengal side, the dividends of any company would be eaten up by the expenses of English or country-bred clerks. The Babu is a great man, and, to respect him, you must see five score or so of him in a room a hundred yards long bending over ledgers, ledgers, and yet more ledgers—silent as the Sphinx and busy as a bee. He is the lubricant of the great machinery of the Company whose ways and works cannot be dealt with in a single scrawl.

CHAPTER II

THE MIGHTY SHOPS

A STUDY of this Republic of Jamalpur is not easy. The railway folk, like the army and civilian castes, have their own language and life, which an outsider cannot hope to understand. For instance, when Jamalpur refers to itself as being "on the long siding," a lengthy explanation is necessary before the visitor grasps the fact that the whole of the two hundred and thirty odd miles of the loop from Luckeeserai to Kanu-Junction *via* Bhagalpur is thus contemptuously treated. Jamalpur insists that it is out of the world, and makes this an excuse for being proud of itself and all its institutions. But in one thing it is badly, disgracefully provided. At a moderate estimate there must be about two hundred Europeans with their families in this place. They can, and do, get their small supplies from Calcutta, but they are dependent on the tender mercies of the bazar for their meat, which seems to be hawked from door to door. Also, there is a Raja who owns or has an interest in the land on which the station stands, and he is averse to cow-killing. For these reasons, Jamalpur is not too well supplied with good meat, and what it wants is a decent meat-market with cleanly controlled slaughtering arrangements. The "Company," who gives grants to the schools and builds the institute and throws the shadow of its protection all over the place, might help this scheme forward.

The heart of Jamalpur is the "shops," and here a visitor will see more things in an hour than he can understand in a year. Steam Street very appropriately leads to the forty or fifty acres that the "shops" cover, and to the busy silence of the loco. superintendent's office, where a man must put down his name and his business on a slip of paper before he can penetrate into the Temple of Vulcan. About three thousand five hundred men are in the "shops," and, ten minutes after the day's work has begun, the assistant superintendent knows exactly how many are "in." The heads of departments—silent, heavy-handed men, captains of five hundred or more—have their names fairly printed on a board which is exactly like a pool-marker. They "star a life" when they come in, and their few names alone represent salaries to the extent of six thousand a month. They are men worth hearing deferentially. They hail from Manchester and the Clyde, and the great ironworks of the North, and pleasant as cold water in a thirsty land is it to hear again the full

Northumbrian burr or the long-drawn Yorkshire "aye." Under their great gravity of demeanor—a man who is in charge of a few lakhs' worth of plant cannot afford to be riotously mirthful—lurks melody and humor. They can sing like north-countrymen, and in their hours of ease go back to the speech of the iron countries they have left behind, when "Ab o' th' yate" and all "Ben Briarly's" shrewd wit shakes the warm air of Bengal with deep-chested laughter. Hear "Ruglan' Toon," with a chorus as true as the fall of trip-hammers, and fancy that you are back again in the smoky, rattling, ringing North.

But this is the "unofficial" side. Let us go forward through the gates under the mango trees, and set foot at once in sheds which have as little to do with mangoes as a locomotive with Lakshmi. The "buzzer" howls, for it is nearly tiffin time. There is a rush from every quarter of the shops, a cloud of flying natives, and a procession of more sedately pacing Englishmen, and in three short minutes you are left absolutely alone among arrested wheels and belts, pulleys, cranks, and cranes—in a silence only broken by the soft sigh of a far-away steam-valve or the cooing of pigeons. You are, by favor freely granted, at liberty to wander anywhere you please through the deserted works. Walk into a huge, brick-built, tin-roofed stable, capable of holding twenty-four locomotives under treatment, and see what must be done to the Iron Horse once in every three years if he is to do his work well. On reflection, Iron Horse is wrong. An engine is a she—as distinctly feminine as a ship or a mine. Here stands the *Echo,* her wheels off, resting on blocks, her underside machinery taken out, and her side scrawled with mysterious hieroglyphics in chalk. An enormous green-painted iron marness-rack bears her piston and eccentric rods, and a neatly-painted board shows that such and such Englishmen are the fitter, assistant and apprentice engaged in editing the *Echo.* An engine seen from the platform and an engine viewed from underneath are two very different things. The one is as unimpressive as a *ticca-gharri;* the other as imposing as a man-of-war in the yard.

In this manner is an engine treated for navicular, laminitis, backsinew, or whatever it is that engines most suffer from. No. 607, we will say, goes wrong at Dinapore, Assensole, Buxar, or whatever it may be, after three years' work. The place she came from is stencilled on the boiler, and the foreman examines her. Then he fills in a hospital sheet, which bears one hundred and eighty printed heads under which an engine can come into the shops. No. 607 needs repair in only one hundred and eighteen particulars, ranging from mud-hole flanges and blower-cocks to lead-plugs, and platform brackets which have shaken loose. This certificate the foreman signs, and it is framed near the engine for the benefit of the three Europeans and the eight or nine natives who have to mend No. 607. To the ignorant the superhuman wisdom of the examiner seems only equalled by the audacity of the two men and the boy who are to undertake what is frivolously called the "job." No. 607 is in a sorely mangled condition, but 403 is much worse. She is reduced to a shell—is a very lean woman of an engine, bearing only her funnel, the iron frame and the saddle that supports the boiler. All the pretty little instruction primers say that an engine takes to pieces like a watch, but it is not good to see an engine so treated. Better had a man believe that "they light the fire under the water, y'know, and that makes the water steam, and that gets into those piston things, and that drives the train."

Four-and-twenty engines in every stage of decomposition stand in one huge shop. A traveling crane runs overhead, and the men have hauled up one end of a bright vermilion loco. The effect is the silence of a scornful stare—just such a look as a colonel's portly wife gives through her *pince-nez* at the audacious subaltern. Engines are the "liveliest" things that man ever made. They glare through their spectacle-plates, they tilt their noses contemptuously, and when their insides are gone they adorn themselves with red lead and leer like decayed beauties; and in the Jamalpur works there is no escape from them. The shops can hold fifty without pressure, and on occasion as many again. Everywhere there are engines, and everywhere brass domes lie about on the ground like huge helmets in a pantomime. The silence is the weirdest touch of all. Some sprightly soul—an apprentice be sure—has daubed in red lead on the end of an iron tool box a caricature of some friend who is evidently a riveter. The picture has all the interest of an Egyptian cartouche, for it shows that men have been here, and that the engines do not have it all their own way.

And so, out in the open, away from the three great sheds between and under more engines, till we strike a wilderness of lines all converging to one turn-table. Here be elephant stalls ranged round a half-circle, and in each stall stands one engine, and each engine stares at the turn-table. A stolid and disconcerting company is this ring of eyed monsters; 324, 432, and 8 are shining like Bon Marche toys. They are ready for their turn of duty, and are as spruce as hansoms. Lacquered chocolate, picked out with black, red and white, is their dress, and delicate lemon graces the ceilings of the cabs. The driver should be a gentleman in evening dress with white kid gloves, and there should be gold-headed champagne bottles in the spick and span tenders. Huckleberry Finn says of a timber raft: "It amounted to something being captain of that raft." Thrice enviable is the man who, drawing Rs. 220 a month, is allowed to make Rs. 150 overtime out of locos. Nos. 324, 432 or 8. Fifty yards beyond this gorgeous trinity are ten to twelve engines who have put in to Jamalpur to bait. They are alive, their fires are lighted, and they are swearing and purring and growling one at another as they stand alone—all alone. Here is evidently one of the newest type—No. 25, a giant who has just brought the mail in and waits to be cleaned up preparatory to going out afresh.

The tiffin hour has ended. The buzzer blows, and with a roar, a rattle and a clang the shops take up their toil. The hubbub that followed on the prince's kiss to the sleeping beauty was not so loud or sudden. Experience, with a foot-rule in his pocket, authority in his port, and a merry twinkle in his eye, comes up and catches Ignorance walking gingerly round No. 25. "That's one of the best we have," says Experience, "a four-wheeled coupled bogie they call her. She's by Dobbs. She's done her hundred and fifty miles to-day; and she'll run in to Rampore Haut this afternoon; then she'll rest a day and be cleaned up. Roughly, she does her three hundred miles in the four-and-twenty hours. She's a beauty. She's out from home, but we can build our own engines—all except the wheels. We're building ten locos. now, and we've got a dozen boilers ready if you care to look at them. How long does a loco. last? That's just as may be. She will do as much as her driver lets her. Some men play the mischief with a loco. and some handle 'em properly. Our drivers prefer Hawthorne's old four-wheel coupled engines because they give the least bother. There is one in that shed, and it's a good 'un to travel. But 80,000 miles generally sees the gloss off an engine, and she goes into the shops to be overhauled and re-fitted and re-planed, and a lot of things that you wouldn't understand if I told you about them. No. 1, the first loco. on the line, is running still, but very little of the original engine must be left by this time. That one there, called the *Fawn*, came out in the Mutiny year. She's by Slaughter and Grunning, and she's built for speed in front of a light load. French-looking sort of thing, isn't she? That's because her cylinders are on a tilt. We used her for the mail once, but the mail has grown heavier and heavier, and now we use six-wheel coupled eighteen inch, inside cylinder, 45-ton locos. to shift thousand-ton trains. *No!* All locos. aren't alike. It isn't merely pulling a lever. The company likes its drivers to know their locos., and a man will keep his Hawthorne for two or three years. The more mileage he gets out of her before she has to be overhauled the better man he is. It pays to let a man have his fancy engine. The Company knows that. Other lines don't. There's the ——. They run the life out of the men and the locos. together. They'll run an engine into the cleaning shed wherever it may be, and then another driver jumps on and runs her back again, and so on till they've run the inside out of her. The drivers don't care. 'Tisn't *their* engine? The other man always said to have damaged her, and so the —— get their stock into a sweet state. 'Come in with a slide bar about red hot, and everything else to match. A man must take an interest in his loco., and that means she must belong to him. Some locos. won't do anything, even if you coax and humor them. I don't *think* there are any unlucky ones now, but some years ago No. 31 wasn't popular. The drivers went sick or took leave when they were told off for her. She killed her driver on the Jubbulpore line, she left the rails at Kajra, she did something or other at Rampur Haunt, and Lord knows what she didn't do or try to do in other places! All the drivers fought shy of her, and in the end she disappeared. They said she was condemned, but I shouldn't wonder if the Company changed her number quietly, and changed the luck at the same time. You see, the Government Inspector comes and looks at our stock now and again, and when an engine's condemned he puts his dhobi mark on her, and she's broken up. Well, No. 31 was condemned, but there was a whisper that they only shifted her number, and ran her out again. When the drivers didn't know there were no accidents. I don't think we've got an unlucky one running now. Some are different from others, but there are no man-eaters. Yes, a driver of the mail *is* somebody. He can make Rs. 370 a month if he's a covenanted man. We get a lot of our drivers in the country, and we don't import from England as much as we did. Stands to reason that, now there's more competition both among lines and in the labor market, the Company can't afford to be as generous as it used to be. It doesn't trap a man though. It's this way with the drivers. A native driver gets about Rs. 20 a month, and in his way he's supposed to be good enough for branch work and shunting and such. Well, an English driver'll get from Rs. 80 to Rs. 220, and overtime. The English driver knows what the native gets, and in time they tell the driver that the native'll improve. The driver has that to think of. You see? That's competition! A driver, one day with another, does his hundred miles a day. Say a man leaves Buxar at 2 p. m. he gets to Allahabad at 7 p. m. That's 163 miles. He rests at Allahabad till 8:20 next morning, when he goes back to Buxar, and rests till about 2 p. m. the next day. Then goes to Mokameh, reaches Mokameh at 7 p. m., stays till 4 next morning, and gets back to Buxar at 9:20 a. m. Then it all begins over again. He has got about three thousand pounds' worth of the Company's property to look after under his own hand, and the Lord knows how much value in the train behind him. Oh, he's got quite enough to think of when he's on his engine."

Experience returns to the engine-sheds, now full of clamor, and enlarges on the beauties of sick locomotives. The fitters and the assistants and the apprentices are hammering and punching and gauging, and otherwise technically disporting themselves round their enormous patients, and their language, as caught in snatches, is beautifully unintelligible.

But one flying sentence goes straight to the heart. It is the cry of humanity over the task of life, done into unrefined English. An apprentice, grimed to his eyebrows, his cloth cap well on the back of his curly head and his hands deep in his pockets, is sitting on the edge of a tool-box ruefully regarding the very much disorganized engine whose slave is he. A handsome boy, this apprentice, and well made. He whistles softly between his teeth and his brow puckers. Then he addresses the engine, saying, half in expostulation and half in despair: "Oh, you condemned old female dog!" He puts the sentence more crisply—much more crisply—and Ignorance chuckles sympathetically.

Ignorance also is puzzled over these engines.

CHAPTER III

AT VULCAN'S FORGE

In the wilderness of the railway shops—and machinery that planes and shaves, and bevels and stamps, and punches and hoists and nips—the first idea that occurs to an outsider, when he has seen the men who people the place, is that it must be the birthplace of inventions—a pasture-ground of fat patents. If a writing-man, who plays with shadows and dresses dolls that others may laugh at their antics, draws help and comfort and new methods of working old ideas from the stored shelves of a library, how, in the name of Commonsense, his god, can a doing-man, whose mind is set upon things that snatch a few moments from flying Time or put power into weak hands, refrain from going forward and adding new inventions to the hundreds among which he daily moves?

Appealed to on this subject, Experience, who had served the E. I. R. loyally for many years, held his peace. "We don't go in much for patents; but," he added, with a praiseworthy attempt to turn the conversation, "we can build you any mortal thing you like. We've got the

Bradford Leslie for the Sahibgunge ferry. Come and see the brass-work for her bows. It's in the casting-shed."

It would have been cruel to have pressed Experience further, and Ignorance, to foredate matters a little, went about to discover why Experience shied off this question, and why the men of Jamalpur had not each and all invented and patented something. He won his information in the end, but did not come from Jamalpur. *That* must be clearly understood. It was found anywhere you please between Howrah and Hoti Mardan; and here it is that all the world may admire a prudent and far-sighted Board of Directors. Once upon a time, as every one in the profession knows, two men invented the D. and O. sleeper—cast iron, of five pieces, very serviceable. The men were in the Company's employ, and their masters said: "Your brains are ours. Hand us over those sleepers." Being of pay and position, D. and O. made some sort of resistance and got a royalty or a bonus. At any rate, the Company had to pay for its sleepers. But thereafter, and the condition exists to this day, they caused it to be written in each servant's covenant, that if by chance he invented aught, his invention was to belong to the Company. Providence has mercifully arranged that no man or syndicate of men can buy the "holy spirit of man" outright without suffering in some way or another just as much as the purchase. America fully, and Germany in part, recognizes this law. The E. I. Railway's breach of it is thoroughly English. They say, or it is said of them, that they say: "We are afraid of our men, who belong to us waking and sleeping, wasting their time on trying to invent."

It is wholly impossible, then, for men of mechanical experience and large sympathies to check the mere patent-hunter and bring forward the man with an idea? Is there no supervision in the "shops," or have the men who play tennis and billiards at the institute not a minute which they can rightly call their very own? Would it ruin the richest Company in India to lend their model shop and their lathes to half-a-dozen, or, for the matter of that, half-a-hundred, abortive experiments? A Massachusetts organ factory, a Racine buggy shop, an Oregon lumber yard would laugh at the notion. An American toy-maker might swindle an *employee* after the invention, but he would in his own interests help the man to "see what comes of the thing." Surely a wealthy, a powerful and, as all Jamalpur bears witness, a considerate Company might cut that clause out of the covenant and await the issue. There would be quite enough jealousy between man and man, grade and grade, to keep down all the keenest souls; and with due respect to the steam-hammer and the rolling-mill, we have not yet made machinery perfect. The "shops" are not likely to spawn unmanageable Stephensons or grasping Brunels; but in the minor turns of mechanical thought that find concrete expressions in links, axle-boxes, joint-packings, valves and spring-stirrups something might—something would—be done were the practical prohibition removed. Will a North countryman give you anything but warm hospitality for nothing? Or if you claim from him overtime service as a right, will he fall to work zealously? "Onything but t' brass," is his motto, and his ideas are his "brass."

Gentlemen in authority, if this should meet your august eyes, spare it a minute's thought, and, clearing away the floridity, get to the heart of the mistake and see if it cannot be rationally put right. Above all, remember that Jamalpur supplied no information. It was as mute as an oyster. There is no one within your jurisdiction to—ahem—"drop upon."

Let us, after this excursion into the offices, return to the shops and only ask Experience such questions as he can without disloyalty answer.

"We used once," says he, leading to the foundry, "to sell our old rails and import new ones. Even when we used 'em for roof beams and so on, we had more than we knew what to do with. Now we have got rolling-mills, and we use the rails to make tie-bars for the D. and O. sleepers and all sorts of things. We turn out five hundred D. and O. sleepers a day. Altogether, we use about seventy-five tons of our own iron a month here. Iron in Calcutta costs about five-eight a hundredweight; ours cost between three-four and three-eight, and on that item alone we save three thousand a month. Don't ask me how many miles of rails we own. There are fifteen hundred miles of line, and you can make your own calculation. All those things like babies' graves, down in that shed, are the moulds of the D. and O. sleepers. We test them by dropping three hundredweight and three hundred quarters of iron on top of them from a height of seven feet, or eleven sometimes. They don't often smash. We have a notion here that our iron is as good as the home stuff."

A sleek, white and brindled pariah thrusts himself into the conversation. His home appears to be on the warm ashes of the bolt-maker. This is a horrible machine, which chews red-hot iron bars and spits them out perfect bolts. Its manners are disgusting, and it gobbles over its food.

"Hi, Jack!" says Experience, stroking the interloper, "you've been trying to break your leg again. That's the dog of the works. At least he makes believe that the works belong to him. He'll follow any one of us about the shops as far as the gate, but never a step further. You can see he's first-class condition. The boys give him his ticket, and, one of these days, he'll try to get on to the Company's books as a regular worker. He's too clever to live." Jack heads the procession as far as the walls of the rolling-shed and then returns to his machinery room. He waddles with fatness and despises strangers.

"How would you like to be hot-potted there?" says Experience, who has read and who is enthusiastic over *She,* as he points to the great furnaces whence the slag is being dragged out by hooks. "Here is the old material going into the furnace in that big iron bucket. Look at the scraps of iron. There's an old D. and O. sleeper, there's a lot of clips from a cylinder, there's a lot of snipped-up rails, there's a driving-wheel block, there's an old hook, and a sprinkling of boiler-plates and rivets."

The bucket is tipped into the furnace with a thunderous roar and the slag below pours forth more quickly. "An engine," says Experience, reflectively, "can run over herself so to say. After she's broken up she is made into sleepers for the line. You'll see how she's broken up later." A few paces further on, semi-nude demons are capering over strips of glowing hot iron which are put into a mill as rails and emerge as thin, shapely tie-bars. The natives wear rough sandals and some pretence of aprons, but the greater part of them is "all face." "As I said before," says Experience, "a native's cuteness when he's working on ticket is something startling. Beyond occasionally hanging on to a red-hot bar too long and so letting their pincers be drawn through the mills, these men take precious good care not to go wrong. Our machinery is fenced and guard-railed as much as possible, and these men don't get caught up by the belting. In the first place, they're careful—the father warns the son and so on—and in the second, there's nothing about 'em for the belting to catch on unless the man shoves his hand in. Oh, a native's no fool! He knows that it doesn't do to be foolish when he's dealing with a crane or a driving-wheel. You're looking at all those chopped rails? We make our iron as they blend baccy. We mix up all sorts to get the required quality. Those rails have just been chopped by this tobacco-cutter thing." Experience bends down and sets a vicious-looking, parrot-headed beam to work. There is a quiver—a snap—and a dull smash and a heavy 76-pound rail is nipped in two like a stick of barley-sugar.

Elsewhere, a bull-nosed hydraulic cutter is rail cutting as if it enjoyed the fun. In another shed stand the steam-hammers; the unemployed ones murmuring and muttering to themselves, as is the uncanny custom of all steam-souled machinery. Experience, with his hand on a long lever, makes one of the monsters perform: and though Ignorance knows that a man designed and men do continually build steam hammers, the effect is as though Experience were maddening a chained beast. The massive block slides down the guides, only to pause hungrily an inch above the anvil, or restlessly throb through a foot and a half of space, each motion being controlled by an almost imperceptible handling of the levers. "When these things are newly overhauled, you can regulate your blow to within an eighth of an inch," says Experience. "We had a foreman here once who could work 'em beautifully. He had the touch. One day a visitor, no end of a swell in a tall, white hat, came round the works, and our foreman borrowed the hat and brought the hammer down just enough to press the knap and no more. 'How wonderful!' said the visitor, putting his hand carelessly upon this lever rod here." Experience suits the action to the word and the hammer thunders on the anvil. "Well you can guess for yourself. Next minute there wasn't enough left of that tall, white hat to make a postage-stamp of. Steam-hammers aren't things to play with. Now we'll go over to the stores and see what happens to the old stock."

Experience leads the way to the Golgotha of Jamalpur. A great tripod, whence depends a pulley, chain, and hook, hangs over a circular fence, strong as an elephant stockade. Inside the stockade is a pit some ten feet deep and twelve or fourteen in diameter. The logs that shore its sides are scarred and bruised and dented and splintered in horrible fashion: even the timbers of the stockade bear the marks of manglement, and at the bottom of the pit lie two enormous iron balls, each nearly a ton's weight, and each bearing a handle. One look at the tripod and chain above and a rent cylinder below explains everything. A row of hopelessly decayed engines and tenders are the "subjects" of this grim dissecting-room. "You see," says Experience, "they hook on one of these balls to that chain, and haul it up by the winch in that fenced shed. Then they drop it on whatever is to be broken up, and—well, they dropped it upon that cylinder, and you can see for yourself what happened. Now, it has often struck me that Rider Haggard might use this place for a sort of variety entertainment, you know. No need to put a man in the pit. Just keep him inside the stockade when the ball fell, and let him dodge the splinters. A shell would be a joke to it. We break up old cannons here. There's the breach of one of them, but some are so curious I've saved them and mounted 'em yonder. They look neat on the red gravel by that fountain—don't they?"

Whatever apparent disorder there might have been in the works, the store department is as clean as a new pin, and stupefying in its naval order. Copper plates, bar, angle, and rod iron, duplicate cranks and slide bars, the piston rods of the *Bradford Leslie* steamer, engine grease, files and hammer-heads—every conceivable article, from leather laces of beltings to head-lamps, necessary for the due and proper working of a long line, is stocked, stacked, piled, and put away in appropriate compartments. In the midst of it all, neck deep in ledgers and indent forms, stands the many-handed Babu, the steam of the engine whose power extends from Howrah to Ghaziabad.

One small set of pigeon-holes contains the bulk of the daily correspondence. It is noticeable that "Sir Bradford Leslie" has a pigeon-hole all to himself. A surreptitious grab at one paper shows that a sergeant-instructor of volunteers, four hundred miles away, has had something done to his kitchen table. And this department knows all about it? *Wah! Wah!* One can only gape vacantly. The E. I. R. is a great chief.

When it cracks its whip, we stand on our hind legs, and walk round the ring backward. Jamalpur does not say this, but that is the feeling in the air.

The Company does everything, and *knows everything*. The gallant apprentice may be a wild youth with an earnest desire to go occasionally "upon the bend." But three times a week, between 7 and 8 p. m., he must attend the night-school and sit at the feet of M. Bonnaud, who teaches him mechanics and statistics so thoroughly that even the awful Government Inspector is pleased. And when there is no night-school the Company will by no means wash its hands of its men out of working-hours. No man can be violently restrained from going to the bad if he insists upon it, but in the service of the Company a man has every warning; his escapades are known, and a judiciously-arranged transfer sometimes keeps a good fellow clear of the downgrade. No one can flatter himself that in the multitude he is overlooked, or believe that between 4 p. m. and 9 a. m. he is at liberty to misdemean himself. Sooner or later, but generally sooner, his goings-on are known, and he is reminded that "Britons never shall be slaves"—to things that destroy good work as well as souls. Maybe the Company acts only in its own interest, but the result is good.

Best and prettiest of the many good and pretty things in Jamalpur is the institute of a Saturday when the Volunteer Band is playing and the tennis courts are full and the babydom of Jamalpur—fat, sturdy children—frolic round the bandstand. The people dance—but big as the institute is, it is getting too small for their dances—they act, they play billiards, they study their newspapers, they play cards and everything else, and they flirt in a sumptuous building, and in the hot weather the gallant apprentice ducks his friend in the big swimming-bath. Decidedly the railway folk make their lives pleasant.

Let us go down southward to the big Giridih collieries and see the coal that feeds the furnace that smelts the iron that makes the sleeper that bears the loco. that pulls the carriage that holds the freight that comes from the country that is made richer by the Great Company Bahadur, the East Indian Railway.

PART THIRD

CHAPTER I

ON THE SURFACE

SOUTHWARD, always southward and easterly, runs the Calcutta Mail from Luckeeserai, till she reaches Madapur in the Sonthal Parganas. From Madapur a train, largely made up of coal-trucks, heads westward into the Hazaribagh district and toward Giridih. A week would not have exhausted "Jamalpur and its environs," as the guide-books say. But since time drives and man must e'en be driven, the weird, echoing bund in the hills above Jamalpur, where the owls hoot at night and hyenas come down to laugh over the grave of "Qullem Roberts, who died from the effects of an encounter with a tiger near this place, A. D. 1864," goes undescribed. Nor is it possible to deal with Monghyr, the head-quarters of the district, where one sees for the first time the age of old Bengal in the sleepy, creepy station, built in a time-eaten fort, which runs out into the Ganges, and is full of quaint houses, with fat-legged balustrades on the roofs. Pensioners certainly, and probably a score of ghosts, live in Monghyr. All the country seems haunted. Is there not at Pir Bahar a lonely house on a bluff, the grave of a young lady, who, thirty years ago, rode her horse down the *khud* and perished? Has not Monghyr a haunted house in which tradition say skeptics have seen much more than they could account for? And is it not notorious throughout the countryside that the seven miles of road between Jamalpur and Monghyr are nightly paraded by tramping battalions of spectres, phantoms of an old-time army massacred, who but Sir W. W. Hunter knows how long ago? The common voice attests all these things, and an eerie cemetery packed with blackened, lichened, candle-extinguished tombstones persuades the listener to believe all that he hears. Bengal is second—or third is it?—in order of seniority among the Provinces, and like an old nurse, she tells many witch-tales.

But ghosts have nothing to do with collieries, and that ever-present "Company," the E. I. R., has more or less made Giridih—principally more. "Before the E. I. R. came," say the people, "we had one meal a day. Now we have two." Stomachs do not tell fibs, whatever mouths may say. That "Company," in the course of business, throws about five lakhs a year into the Hazaribah district in the form of wages alone, and Giridih Bazar has to supply the wants of twelve thousand men, women and children. But we have now the authority of a number of high-souled and intelligent native prints that the Sahib of all grades spends his time in "sucking the blood out of the country," and "flying to England to spend his ill-gotten gains." It is curious to watch a Sahib engaged in this operation. He —but no matter. His way shall be dealt with later on.

Giridih is perfectly mad—quite insane! Geologically, the big, thick books show that the country is in the metamorphic higher grounds that rise out of the alluvial flats of Lower Bengal between the Osri and the Barakar rivers. Translated, this sentence means that you can twist your ankle on pieces of pure white, pinky and yellowish granite, slip over weather-worn sandstone, grievously cut your boots over flakes of trap, and throw hornblende pebbles at the dogs. Never was such a place for stone-throwing as Giridih. The general aspect of the country is falsely park-like, because it swells and sings in a score of grass-covered undulations, and is adorned with plantation-like *sal* jungle. There are low hills on every side, and twelve miles away bearing south the blue bulk of the holy hills of Parasnath, greatest of the Jain Tirthankars, overlooks the world. In Bengal they consider four thousand five hundred feet good enough for a Dagshai or Kasauli, and once upon a time tried to put troops on Parasnath. There was a scarcity of water, and Thomas of those days found the silence and seclusion prey upon his spirits. Since twenty years, therefore, Parasnath has been abandoned by Her Majesty's Army.

As to Giridih itself, the last few miles of train bring up the reek of the "Black Country." Memory depends on smell. A noseless man is devoid of sentiment, just as a noseless woman, in this country, must be devoid of honor. That first breath of the coal should be the breath of the murky, clouded tract between Yeadon and Dale—or Barnsley, rough and hospitable Barnsley—or Dewsbury and Batley and the Derby Canal, on a Sunday afternoon when the wheels are still and the young men and maidens walk stolidly in pairs. Unfortunately, it is nothing more than Giridih—seven thousand miles away from home and blessed with a warm and genial sunshine, soon to turn into something very much worse. The insanity of the place is visible at the station door. A G. B. T. cart once married a bathing-machine, and they called the child *tum-tum*. You who in flannel and Cawnpore harness drive bamboo-carts about up-country roads, remember that a Giridih *tum-tum* is painfully pushed by four men, and must be entered crawling on all-fours, head first. So strange are the ways of Bengal.

"They drive mad horses in Giridih—animals

that become hysterical as soon as the dusk falls and the countryside blazes with the fires of the great coke ovens. If you expostulate tearfully, they produce another horse, a raw, red fiend whose ear has to be screwed round and round, and round and round, in a twitch before she will by any manner of means, consent to start. Also, the roads carry neat little eighteen inch trenches at their sides, admirably adapted to hold the flying wheel. Skirling about this savage land in the dark, the white population beguile the time by rapturously recounting past accidents, insisting throughout on the super-equine "steadiness" of their cattle. Deep and broad and wide is their jovial hospitality; but somebody—the Tirhoot planters for choice—ought to start a mission to teach the men of Giridih what to drive. They know how, or they would be severally and separately and many times dead, but they do not. they do not indeed, know that animals who stand on one hind leg and beckon with all the rest, or try to pikstick in harness, are not trap-horses worthy of endearing names, but things to be pole-axed. Their feelings are hurt when you say this. "Sit tight," say the men of Giridih; "we're insured! We can't be hurt."

And now with grey hairs, dry mouth, and chattering teeth to the colliers. The E. I. R. estate, bought or leased in perpetuity from the

Serampore Raja, may be about four miles long and between one and two miles across. It is in two pieces, the Serampore field being separated from Karharbari (or Kurhurballi or Kabarbari) field by the property of the Bengal Coal Company. The Raneegunge Coal Association lies to the east of all other workings. So we have three companies at work on about eleven square miles of land.

There is no such thing as getting a full view of the whole place. A short walk over a grassy down gives on to an outcrop of very dirty sandstone, which in the excessive innocence of their hearts most visitors will naturally take to be the coal lying neatly on the surface. Up to this sandstone the path seems to be made of crushed sugar, so white and shiny is the quartz. Over the brow of the down comes in sight the old familiar pit-head wheel, spinning for the dear life, and the eye loses itself in a maze of pumping sheds, red-tiled, mud-walled miners' huts, dotted all over the landscape and railway lines that seem to run on every kind of gradient. There are lines that dip into valleys and disappear round the shoulders of slopes, and lines that career on the tops of rises and disappear over the brow of the slopes. Along these lines whistle and pant metre-gauge engines, some with trucks at their tail and others rattling back to the pit-bank with the absurd air of a boy late for school that an unemployed engine always assumes. There are six engines in all, and as it is easiest to walk along the lines one sees a good deal of them. They bear not altogether unfamiliar names. Here, for instance, passes the "Cockburn" whistling down a grade with thirty tons of coal at her heels; while the "Whitly" and the "Olpherts" are waiting for their complements of trucks. Now a Mr. T. F. Cockburn was superintendent of these mines nearly thirty years ago, in the days before the chord lines from Kanu to Luckeeserai was built, and all the coal was carted to the latter place: and surely Mr. Olpherts was an engineer who helped to think out a new sleeper. What may these things mean?

"Apotheosis of the manager," is the reply. "Christen the engines after the managers. You'll find Cockburn, Dunn, Whitly, Abbott, Olpherts and Saise knocking about the place. Sounds funny, doesn't it? Doesn't sound so funny, when one of these idiots does his best to derail Saise, though, by putting a line down anyhow. Look at that line! Laid out in knots—by Jove!" To the unprofessional eye the rails seem all correct; but there must be something wrong, because "one of those idiots" is asked why in the name of all he considers sacred he does not ram the ballast properly.

"What would happen if you threw an engine off the line?" "Can't say that I know exactly. You see, our business is to keep them *on*, and we do that. Here's rather a curiosity. You see that pointsman! They say he's an old mutineer, and when he relaxes he boasts of the Sahibs he has killed. He's glad enough to eat the Company's salt now." Such a withered old face was the face of the pointsman at No. 11 point! The information suggested a host of questions, and the answers were these: "You won't be able to understand till you've been down into a mine. We work our men in two ways: some by direct payment—*sirkari*—under our own hand, and some by contractors. The contractor undertakes to deliver us the coal, supplying his own men, tools and props. He's responsible for the safety of his men, and of course the Company knows and sees his work. Just fancy, among these five thousand people, what sort of effect the *khuber* of an accident would produce! It would go all through the Sonthal Parganas. We have any amount of Sonthal besides Mahomedans and Hindus of every possible caste, down to those Musahers who eat pig. They don't require much administering in the civilian sense of the word. On Sundays, as a rule, if any man has had his daughter eloped with, or anything of that kind, he generally comes up to the manager's bungalow to get the matter put straight. If a man is disabled through accident he knows that as long as he's in the hospital he gets full wages, and the Company pays for the food of any of his women-folk who come to look after him. One of course: not the whole clan. That makes our service popular with the people—poor beggars. Don't you believe that a native is a fool. You can train him to everything except responsibility. There's a rule in the workings that if there is any dangerous work, no—we haven't choke damps, I will show you when we get down—no gang must work without an Englishman to look after them. A native wouldn't be wise enough to understand what the danger was, or where it came in. Even if he did, he'd shirk the responsibility. We can't afford to risk a single life. All our output is just as much as the Company want—about a thousand tons per working day. Three hundred thousand in the year. We could turn out more? Yes—a little. Well, yes, twice as much. I won't go on, because you wouldn't believe me. There's the coal under us, and we work it at any depth from following up an outcrop down to six hundred feet. That is our deepest shaft. We have no necessity to go deeper. At home the mines are sometimes fifteen hundred feet down. Well, the thickness of this coal here varies from anything you please to anything you please. There's enough of it to last your time and one or two hundred years longer. Perhaps even longer than that. Look at that stuff. That's big coal from the pit."

It was aristocratic-looking coal, just like the picked lumps that are stacked in baskets of coal agencies at home with the printed legend atop "only *23s* a ton." But there was no picking in this case. The great piled banks were all "equal to samples," and beyond them lay piles of small, broken, "smithy" coal. "The Company doesn't sell to the public. This small, broken coal is an exception. That is sold, but the big stuff is for the engines and the shops. It doesn't cost much to get out, as you say; but our men can earn as much as twelve rupees a month. Very often when they've earned enough to go on with they retire from the concern till they've spent their money and then come on again. It's piecework and they are improvident. If some of them only lived like other natives they would have enough to buy land and cows with. When there's a press of work they make a good deal by overtime, but they don't seem to keep it. You should see Giridih Bazar on a Sunday if you want to know where the money goes. About ten thousand rupees change hands once a week there. If you want to get at the number of people who are indirectly dependent or profit by the E. I. R.

you'll have to conduct a census of your own. After Sunday is over the men generally lie off on Monday and take it easy on Tuesday. Then they work hard for the next four days and make it up. Of course there's nothing in the wide world to prevent a man from resigning and going away to wherever he came from—behind those hills if he's a Sonthal. He loses his employment, that's all. And they have their own point of honor. A man hates to be told by his friends that he has been guilty of *nimakharami.* And now we'll go to breakfast. You shall be 'pitted' to-morrow to any depth you like."

CHAPTER II

IN THE DEPTHS

"PITTED to any extent you please." The only difficulty was for Joseph to choose his pit. Giridih was full of them. There was an arch in the side of a little hill, a blackened brick arch leading into thick night. A stationary engine was hauling a procession of coal-laden trucks—"tubs" is the technical word—out of its depths. The tubs were neither pretty nor clean. "We are going down in those when they are emptied. Put on your helmet, and *keep* it on and keep your head down." The trucks were unloaded into the wagons of the metre-gauge colliery line in this wise. Drawn out by the engine along the line, they were pulled on to a platform of smooth iron, dexterously swung round by black demons in attendance, and slid on to what is technically termed a "tippler." This is a most crafty arrangement, partaking of the nature of a drop and a safety-stirrup. The tub goes forward until it is brought up by the curved ends of the metals it travels on, and sticks in a sort of gigantic stirrup. Then, gravely and solemnly, it overbalances itself, turns through half a circle, and shoots its load into the big truck below. Some of the "tipplers" are fixed on traveling platforms and can be moved down the whole length of a waiting coal-train. The Ratel—is it not?—is the eccentric beast in the Zoo who runs round his cage and turns head-over-heels at a given place. These absurd tubs are Ratels, and the gravity of their self-arranged somersaults is very comic.

But there is nothing mirth-provoking in going down a coal-mine—even though it be only a shallow incline running to one hundred and forty feet vertical below the earth. "Get into the tub and lie down. Hang it, no! This is not a railway carriage: you can't see the country out of the windows. *Lie down* in the dust and don't lift your head. Let her go!"

The tubs strain on the wire rope and slide down fourteen hundred feet of incline, at first through a chastened gloom, and then through darkness. An absurd sentence from a trial report rings in the head: "About this time prisoner expressed a desire for the consolations of religion." A hand with a reeking flare-lamp hangs over the edge of the tub, and there is a glimpse of a blackened *solah topee* near it, for those accustomed to the pits have a merry trick of going down sitting or crouching on the coupling of the rear tub. The noise is deafening, and the roof is very close indeed. The tubs bump, and the occupant crouches lovingly in the coal dust. What would happen if the train went off the line? The desire for the "consolations of religion" grows keener and keener as the air grows closer and closer. The tubs stop in darkness spangled, not lifted, by the light of the flare-lamps which many black devils carry. Underneath and on both sides there is the greasy blackness of the coal, and, above, a roof of grey sandstone, smooth as the flow of a river at evening. "Now, remember that if you don't keep your *topee* on, you'll get your head broken, because you will forget to stoop. If you hear any tubs coming up behind you step off to one side. There's a tramway under your feet, and be careful not to trip over it."

The miner has a gait as peculiarly his own as Tommy's measured paces or the blue jacket's roll. Big men who slouch in the light of day become almost things of beauty underground. Their foot is on their native heather; and the slouch is a very necessary act of homage to the great earth, which if a man observe not, he shall without doubt have his *solah topee*—bless the man who invented pith hats!—grievously cut and dented, and himself dowered with an aching head.

The road turns and winds and the roof becomes lower, but those accursed tubs still rattle by on the tramways. The roof throws back their noises, and when all the place is full of a grumbling and a growling, how under earth is one to know whence danger will turn up next? Also, the air is choking, and brings about, to the unacclimatized, a singing in the ears, a hotness of the eyeballs, and a jumping of the heart. "That's because the pressure here is different from the pressure up above. It'll wear off in a minute. *We* don't notice it. Wait till you get down a four-hundred-foot pit. *Then* your ears will begin to sing, if you like." Most people know the One Night of each hot weather—that still, clouded night just before the rain breaks, when there seems to be no more breathable air under the bowl of the pitiless skies, and all the weight of the silent, dark house lies on the chest of the sleep-hunter. This is the feeling in a coal-mine—only more so—much more so, for the darkness is the "gross darkness of the inner sepulchre." It is hard to see which is the black coal and which the passage driven through it. From far away, down the side galleries, comes the regular beat of the pick—thick and muffled as the beat of the laboring heart. "Six men to a gang, and they aren't allowed to work alone. They make six-foot drives through the coal—two and sometimes three men working together. The rest clear away the stuff and load it into the tubs. We have no props in this gallery because we have a roof as good as a ceiling. The coal lies under the sandstone here.

It's beautiful sandstone." It *was* beautiful sandstone—as hard as a billiard table and devoid of any nasty little bumps and jags which cut into the hat.

There was a roaring down one road—the roaring of infernal fires. This is not a pleasant thing to hear in the dark. It is too suggestive. "That's our ventilating shaft. Can't you feel the air getting brisker? Come and look."

Imagine a great iron-bound crate of burning coal, hanging over a gulf of darkness faintly showing the brickwork of the base of a chimney. "We're at the bottom of the shaft. That fire makes a draught that sucks up the foul air from the bottom of the pit. There's another down-draw shaft in another part of the mine where the clean air comes in. We aren't going to set the mines on fire. There's an earth and *kutcha* brick floor at the bottom of the pit; the crate hangs over. It isn't so deep as you think." Then a devil—a naked devil—came in with a pitchfork and fed the spouting flames. This was perfectly in keeping with the landscape, but it was not pretty. "That's only a little shaft. We've got one, an oval, eighteen feet by twelve, and four hundred and fifty feet deep. They aren't sunk like wells. Our sandstones are stronger than any bricks. We brick through the twenty feet of surface soil, but we can sink straight through the sandstone, knowing that the sinkings will stand. Now we'll go to the place where they are taking out the coal."

More trucks, more muffled noises, more darkness made visible, and more devils—male and female—coming out of darkness and vanishing. Then a picture to be remembered. A great Hall of Eblis, twenty feet from inky-black floor to grey roof, upheld by huge pillars of shining coal and filled with flitting and passing devils. On a shattered pillar near the roof stood a naked man, his flesh olive-colored in the light of the lamps, hewing down a mass of coal that still clove to the roof. Behind him was the wall of darkness, and when the lamps shifted he disappeared like a ghost. The devils were shouting directions, and the man howled in reply, resting on his pick and wiping the sweat from his brow. When he smote the coal crushed and slid and rumbled from the darkness into the darkness, and the devils cried *shabash!* The man stood erect like a bronze statue, he twisted and bent himself like a Japanese grotesque, and anon threw himself on his side after the manner of the dying gladiator. Then spoke the still small voice of fact: "A first-class workman if he would only stick to it. But as soon as he makes a little money he lies off and spends it. That's the last of a pillar that we've knocked out. See here. These pillars of coal are square, about thirty feet each way. As you can see, we make the pillar first by cutting out all the coal between. Then we drive a square tunnel, about seven feet wide, through and across the pillar, propping it with baulks. There's one fresh cut."

Two tunnels crossing at right angles had been driven through a pillar which in its under-cut condition seemed like the rough draft of a statue for an elephant. "When the pillar stands only on four legs we chip away one leg at a time from a square to an hour-glass shape, and then either the whole of the pillar crashes down from the roof or else a quarter or a half. If the coal lies against the sandstones it carries away clear, but in some places it brings down stone and rubbish with it. The chipped-away legs of the pillars are called stooks." "Who has to make the last cut that breaks a leg through?" "Oh! Englishmen of all sorts. We can't trust natives for the job unless it's very easy. The natives take kindly to the pillar work though. They are paid just as much for their coal as though they had hewed it out of the solid. Of course we take very good care to see that the roof doesn't come in on us. You would never understand how and why we prop our roofs with those piles of sleepers. Anyway, you can see that we cannot take out a whole line of pillars. We work 'em *en echelon*, and those big beams you see running from floor to roof are our indicators. They show when the roof is going to give. Oh! dear no, there's no dramatic effect about it. No splash, you know. Our roofs give plenty of warning by cracking and then *baito* slowly. The parts of the work that we have cleared out and allowed to fall in are called goafs'. You're on the edge of a goaf' now. All that darkness there marks the limit of the mine. We have worked that out piecemeal, and the props are gone and the place is down. The roof of any pillar-working is tested every morning by tapping—pretty hard tapping."

"Hi yi! yi!" shout all the devils in chorus, and the Hall of Eblis is full of rolling sound. The olive man has brought down an *avalanche* of coal. "It is a sight to see the whole of one of the pillars come away. They make an awful noise. It would startle you out of your wits. Some of 'em are ninety feet square. But there's not an atom of risk."

("Not an atom of risk." Oh, genial and courteous host, when you turned up next day blacker than any sweep that ever swept, with a neat, half-inch gash on your forehead—won by cutting a "stook" and getting caught by a bounding coal-knob—how long and earnestly did you endeavor to show that "stook-cutting" was an employment as harmless and unexciting as wool-samplering?)

"If you knew about mining, you'd see that our ways are rather primitive, but they're cheap, and they're safe as houses. Doms and Bauris, Kols and Beldars don't understand refinements in mining. They'd startle an English pit where there was fire-damp. Do you know it's a solemn fact that if you drop a Davy lamp or snatch it quickly you can blow a whole English pit inside out with all the miners? Good for us that we don't know what fire-damp is here. We can use the flare-lamps."

After the first feeling of awe and wonder is worn out, a mine becomes monotonous. How could a mine be anything but monotonous. Mile after mile of blackness stretching before the eyes as far as sight will carry, which is not saying much, even when one has been some time accustomed to the lack of light. There is only the humming, palpitating darkness, the rumble of the tubs and the endless procession of galleries to arrest the attention. And one pit to the uninitiated is as like to another as two peas. Tell a miner this and he laughs—slowly and softly. To him the pits have each distinct personalities, and each must be dealt with a different way. A descent from the pit-bank, and not from the mouth of an incline, is sickening—channel-passage sickening. Over pulley-wheels, mounted on shearlegs thirty, forty, or fifty feet high, passes the wire rope that is fastened to the "cages"—the two lifts on which the empty coal tubs go down and the loaded ones come up. A cage either has wooden guides at the four corners of the shaft or grips wire guide-ropes to steady it as it is let down. An engine drives the drum on which the wire-rope hauling line is coiled.

Very curious is a pit-bank when the work is in full swing. A hammer close to the winding engine strikes one, the driver places his foot on the lever: there is a roar far down the shaft, and an iron-railed platform with the loaded tub on it flies up and settles with a clang on four catches. The tub is run out into a "tippler" and discharges itself into a coal-truck. By the time it is run back empty into the second cage, a loaded truck is made ready at the bottom of the shaft, and as the empty truck sinks the full rises.

The hammer strikes three. The "winder" by the engine pulls the lever thrice, no empty tub is put into the cage, and the speed of the rise is not so great. There springs up a miner. He is a man, if we could get through the coal dust, and on his account special precautions are taken, and woe betide the pit-men who neglect them. All these things are lovely to look at. But the actual descent is not so good. If you swing a child vehemently, the little innocent is likely to complain that he feels as though his "tummy were left in the air." Now this is the exact sensation of dropping into a pit. The hangman adjusts the white cap. That is to say, you cram your hat down and go—drop away from the day and every one you ever loved, *and* your "tummy." That comes down later. You arrive destitute of any inside, and are told for your comfort that in some of the English mines you can go down two thousand feet at the rate of sixty miles an hour. Two hundred feet at a considerably slower rate is enough—quite enough. Try it once or twice, and see what the air is like.

The return journey is said to possess an element of risk. For this reason. If the "winder" of the engine at the top stopped to think, or hunted for a flea, or got a fit, or was choked by a fly, his engine would continue to wind and wind until the cage was hauled up to the pulley-wheels thirty feet in the air, where it would have three courses open to it. It might jam, break the wire rope and fall back unbridled into the pit, or part into several pieces, or be hauled with one tremendous bound right over the pulley-wheels and come down a bundle of shattered ribs. In any case the occupant would not be in a position to describe the precise nature of the accident. But a native "winder" knows these things, and thinks of them every time the three taps come to his ears. For him "over-winding" would mean loss of post and pay. Therefore he does not overwind. He generally has a keen rivalry with a fellow-winder at another pit-bank, and lays himself out to see if he cannot bring more tons of coal to the bank than his *bhai.*

CHAPTER III

THE PERILS OF THE PITS

AN engineer, who has built a bridge, can strike you nearly dead with professional facts; the captain of a seventy horse power Ganges river-steamer can, in one hour, tell legends about the Sandheads and the James and Mary shoal sufficient to fill half a *Pioneer*, but a couple of days spent on, above, and in a coal mine yields more mixed information than two engineers and three captains. It is hopeless to pretend to understand it all.

When your host says: "Ah, such an one is a thundering good fault-reader!" you smile hazily, and by way of keeping up the conversation, adventure on the statement that fault-reading and palmistry are very popular amusements. Then men laugh consumedly, and enter into explanations.

Every one knows that coal strata, in common with women, horses, and official superiors, have "faults" caused by some colic of the earth in the days when things were settling into their places. A coal seam is suddenly sliced off as a pencil is cut through with one slanting blow of the penknife, and one-half is either pushed up or pushed down any number of feet. The miners work the seam till they come to this break-off, and then call for an expert to "read the fault." It is sometimes very hard to discover whether the sliced-off beam has gone up or down. Theoretically, the end of the broken piece should show the direction. Practically its indications are not always clear. Then a good "fault-reader," who must more than know geology, is a useful man, and is much prized, for the Giridih fields are full of faults and "dykes." Tongues of what was once molten lava thrust themselves sheer into the coal, and the disgusted miner finds that for about twenty feet on each side of the tongue all the coal has been burned away.

The head of the mine is supposed to foresee these things and ever so many more. He can tell you, without looking at the map, what is the geological formation of any thousand square miles of India; he knows as much about brick-work and the building of houses, arches, and shafts as an average P. W. D. man; he has not only to know the intestines of a pumping or winding engine, but must be able to take them to pieces with his own hands, indicate on the spot such parts as need repair, and make drawings of anything that requires renewal; he knows how to lay out and build railways with a grade of one in twenty-seven; he has to carry in his head all the signals and points between and over which his locomotive engines work; he has to be an electrician capable of controlling the apparatus that fires the dynamite charges in the pits, and must thoroughly understand boring operations with thousand-foot drills. Over and above this, he must know by name, at least, one thousand of the men on the works, and must fluently speak the vernaculars of the low castes. If he has Sonthali, which is more elaborate than Greek, so much the better for him. He must know how to handle men of all grades, and, while himself holding aloof, must possess sufficient grip of the men's private lives to be able to see at once the merits of a charge of attempted abduction preferred by a clucking, croaking Kol against a fluent English-speaking Brahmin. For he is literally the Light of Justice, and to him the injured husband or the wrathful father looks for redress. He must be on the spot and take all responsibility when any specially risky job is under way in the pit, and he can claim no single hour of the day or the night for his own. From eight in the morning till one in the afternoon he is coated with coal-dust and oil. From one till eight in the evening he has office work. After eight o'clock he is free to attend to anything that he may be wanted for.

This is a soberly-drawn picture of a life that *Sahibs* on the mines actually enjoy. They are spared all private socio-official worry, for the Company, in its mixture of State and private interest, is as perfectly cold-blooded and devoid of bias as any great, grinding Department of the Empire. If certain things be done, well and good. If certain things be not done the defaulter goes, and his place is filled by another. The conditions of service are graven on stone. There may be generosity: there undoubtedly is justice, but above all there is freedom within broad limits. No irrepressible shareholder cripples the executive arm with suggestions and restrictions, and no private piques turn men's blood to gall within them. Therefore men work like horses and are happy.

When he can snatch a free hour, the grimy, sweating, cardigan-jacketed. ammunition-booted, pick-bearing ruffian turns into a well-kept English gentleman, who plays a good game of billiards, and has a batch of new books from England every week. The change is sudden, but in Giridih nothing is startling. It is right and natural that a man should be alternately Valentine and Orson, specially Orson. It is right and natural to drive—always behind a mad horse—away and away toward the lonely hills till the flaming coke ovens become glow-worms on the dark horizon. and in the wilderness to find a lovely English maiden teaching squat, filthy Sonthal girls how to become Christians. Nothing is strange in Giridih, and the stories of the pits, the raffle of conversation that a man picks up as he passes, are quite in keeping with the place. Thanks to the law, which enacts that an Englishman must look after the native miners, and if any be killed, he and he alone has to explain satisfactorily that the accident was not due to preventable causes, the death-roll is kept astoundingly low. In one "bad" half-year six men out of the five thousand were killed, in another four, and in another none at all. Given "butcher bills" as small as these, it is not astonishing that the men in charge do their best to cut them down at any cost of time and sleep. As has been said before, a big accident would scare off the workers, for, in spite of the age of the mines —nearly thirty years—the hereditary pitman has not yet been evolved. But to small accidents the men are orientally apathetic. Be pleased to read of a death among the five thousand.

A gang has been ordered to cut clay for the luting of the coke furnaces. The clay is piled in a huge bank in the open sunlight above ground. A coolie hacks and hacks till he has hewn out a small cave with twenty feet of clay above him. Why should he trouble to climb up the bank and bring down the eave of the cave? It is easier to cut in. The Sirdar of the gang is watching round the shoulder of the bank. The coolie cuts lazily as he stands: Sunday is very near, and he will get gloriously drunk in Giridih Bazar with his week's earnings. He digs his own grave stroke by stroke, for he has not sense enough to see that undercut clay is dangerous. He is a Sonthal from the hills. There is a smash and a dull thud, and his grave has shut down upon him in an *avalanche* of heavy-caked clay.

The Sirdar calls to the Babu of the Ovens, and with the promptitude of his race the Babu loses his head. He runs puffily, without giving orders, anywhere, everywhere Finally he runs to the *Sahib's* house. The *Sahib* is at the other end of the collieries. He runs back. The *Sahib* has gone home to wash. Then his indiscretion strikes him. He should have sent runners—fleet-footed boys from the coal-screening gangs. He sends them and they fly. One catches the *Sahib* just changed after his bath. "There is a man dead at such a place"—he gasps, omitting to say whether it is a surface or a pit accident. On goes the grimy pit kit, and in three minutes the *Sahib's* dogcart is flying to the place indicated.

They have dug out the Sonthal. His head is smashed in, spine and breastbone are broken, and the gang Sirdar, bowing double, throws the blame of the accident on the poor, shapeless, battered dead. "I had warned him, but he would not listen! *Twice* I warned him! These men are witnesses."

The Babu is shaking like a jelly. "Oh, sar, I have never seen a man killed before! Look at that eye, sar! I should have sent runners. I ran everywhere. I ran to your house. You were not in. I was running for hours. It was not my fault! It was the fault of the gang Sirdar." He wrings his hands and gurgles. The best of accountants, but the poorest of coroners is he. No need to ask how the accident happened. No need to listen to the Sirdar and his "witnesses." The Sonthal had been a fool, but it was the Sirdar's business to protect him against his own folly. "Has he any people here?"

"Yes, his *rukni*, his kept-woman, and his sister's brother-in-law. His home is far-off."

The sister's brother-in-law breaks through the crowd howling for vengeance on the Sirdar. He will send for the police, he will have the price of his *bhai's* blood full tale. The windmill arms and the angry eyes fall, for the *Sahib* is making the report of the death.

"Will this Sirkar give me *pensin?* I am his wife," a woman clamors, stamping her pewter-ankleted feet. "He was killed in your service. Where is his *pensin?* I am his wife." "You lie! You're his *rukni*. Keep quiet! Go! The *pensin* comes to *us.*" The sister's brother-in-law is not a refined man, but the *rukni* is his match. They are silenced. The Sahib takes the report, and the body is borne away. Before to-morrow's sun rises the Sirdar may find himself a simple "surface-coolie," earning nine pice a day; and, in a week some Sonthal woman behind the hills may discover that she is entitled to draw monthly great wealth from the coffers of the *Sirkar.* But this will not happen if the sister's brother-in-law can prevent it. He goes off swearing at the *rukni.*

But, in the meantime, what have the rest of the dead man's gang been doing? They have, if you please, abating not one stroke, dug out all the clay, and would have it verified. They have seen their comrade die. He is dead. *Bus!* Will the Sirdar take the tale of clay? And yet, were twenty men to be crushed by their own carelessness in the pit, these impassive workers would scatter like panic-stricken horses.

But, turning from this sketch, let us set in order some of the stories of the pits. These are quaint tales. The miner-folk laugh when they tell them. In some of the mines the coal is blasted out by the dynamite which is fired by electricity from a battery on the surface. Two men place the charges, and then signal to be drawn up in the cage which hangs in the pit-eye. On one occasion two natives were entrusted with the job. They performed their parts beautifully till the end, when the vaster idiot of the two scrambled into the cage, gave signal, and was hauled up before his friend could enter.

Thirty or forty yards up the shaft all possible danger for those in the cage was over, and the charge was accordingly exploded. Then it occurred to the man in the cage that his friend stood a very good chance of being by this time riven to pieces and choked.

But the friend was wise in his generation. He had missed the cage, but found a coal-tub—one of the little iron trucks—and turning this upside down, had crawled into it. His account of the explosion has never been published. When the charge went off, his shelter was battered in so much, that men had to hack him out, for the tub had made, as it were, a tinned sardine of its occupant. He was absolutely uninjured, but his feelings were lacerated. On reaching the pit-bank his first words were: "I do not desire to go down the pit with *that* man any more." His wish had been already gratified for "that man" had fled. Later on, the story goes, when "that man" found that the guilt of murder was not at his door, he returned, and was made a surface-coolie, and his *bhai-band* jeered at him as they passed to their better-paid occupation.

Occasionally there are mild cyclones in the pits. An old working, perhaps a mile away, will collapse: a whole gallery sinking in bodily. Then the displaced air rushes through the inhabited mine, and, to quote their own expression, blows the pitmen about "like dry leaves." Few things are more amusing than the spectacle of a burly Tyne-side foreman who, failing to dodge round a corner in time, is "put down" by the wind, sitting fashion, on a knobby lump of coal.

But most impressive of all is a tale they tell of a fire in a pit many years ago. The coal caught —light. They had to send earth and bricks down the shaft and build great dams across the galleries to choke the fire. Imagine the scene, a few hundred feet underground, with the air growing hotter and hotter each moment, and the carbonic acid gas trickling through the dams. After a time the rough dams gaped, and the gas poured in afresh, and the Englishmen went down and leeped the cracks between roof and dam-sill with anything they could get. Coolies fainted, and had to be taken away, but no one died, and behind the kutcha dams they built great masonry ones, and bested that fire; though for a long time afterward, whenever they pumped water into it, the steam would puff out from crevices in the ground above.

It is a queer life that they lead, these men of

the coal-fields, and a "big" life to boot. To describe one-half of their labors would need a week at the least, and would be incomplete then. "If you want to see anything," they say, "you should go over to the Baragunda copper-mines; you should look at the Barakar ironworks; you should see our boring operations five miles away; you should see how we sink pits; you should, above all, see Giridih Bazar on a Sunday. Why, you haven't seen anything. There's no end of a Sonthal Mission hereabouts. All the little dev—dears have gone on a picnic. Wait till they come back, and see 'em learning to learn."

Alas! one cannot wait. At the most one can but thrust an impertinent pen skin-deep into matters only properly understood by specialists.

PART FOURTH

IN AN OPIUM FACTORY

On the banks of the Ganges, forty miles below Benares as the crow flies, stands the Ghazipur Factory, an opium mint as it were, whence issue the precious cakes that are to replenish the coffers of the Indian Government. The busy season is setting in, for with April the opium comes in from districts after having run the gauntlet of the district officers of the Opium Department, who will pass it as fit for use. Then the really serious work begins under a roasting sun. The opium arrives by *challans,* regiments of one hundred jars, each holding one maund and each packed in a basket and sealed atop. The district officer submits forms—never was such a place for forms as the Ghazipur Factory—showing the quality and weight of each pot, and with the jars come a ziladar responsible for the safe carriage of the *challans,* their delivery and their virginity. If any pots are broken or tampered with an unfortunate individual called the import officer, and appointed to work like a horse from dawn till dewy eve, must examine the ziladar in charge of the *challan* and reduce his statement to writing. Fancy getting any native to explain how a *matka* has been smashed. But the perfect lower is about as valuable as silver.

Then all the pots have to be weighed, and the weights—Calcutta Mint, if you please—and the beams must be daily tested. The weight of each pot is recorded on the pot, in a book, and goodness knows where else, and every one has to sign certificates that the weighing is correct. *Nota bene.* The pots have been weighed once in the district and once in the factory. Therefore a certain number of them are taken at random and weighed afresh before they are opened. This is only the beginning of the long series of checks. All sorts of inquiries are made about light pots, and then the testing begins. Every single, serially-numbered pot has to be tested for quality. A native called the *purkhea* drives his fist into the opium, rubs and smells it, and calls out the class for the benefit of the opium examiner. A sample picked between finger and thumb is thrown into a jar, and if the opium examiner thinks the *purkhea* has said sooth, the class of the jar is marked in chalk, and everything is entered in a book. Every ten samples are put in a locked box with duplicated keys, and sent over to the laboratory for assay. With the tenth boxful—and this marks the end of the *challan* of a hundred jars—the Englishman in charge of the testing signs the test paper, and enters the name of the native tester and sends it over to the laboratory. For convenience sake, it may be as well to say that, unless distinctly stated to the contrary, every single thing in Ghazipur is locked, and every operation is conducted under more than police supervision.

In the laboratory each set of ten samples is thoroughly mixed by hand, a quarter ounce lump is then tested for starch adulteration by iodine which turns the decoction blue, and, if necessary, for gum adulteration by alcohol which makes the decoction filmy. If adulteration be shown, all the ten pots of that set are tested separately. When the sinful pot is discovered, all the opium is tested in four-pound lumps. Over and above this test, three samples of one hundred grains each are taken from the *jummakaroed* set of ten samples, dried on a steam table and then weighed for consistence. The result is written down in a ten-columned form in the assay register, and by the mean result are those ten pots paid for. This, after everything has been done in duplicate and countersigned, completes the test and assay. If a district officer has classed the opium in a glaringly wrong way, he is thus caught and reminded of his error. No one trusts any one in Ghazipur. They are always weighing, testing and assaying.

Before the opium can be used it must be "alligated" in big vats. The pots are emptied into these, and special care is taken that none of the drug sticks to the hands of the coolies. Opium has a special knack of doing this, and therefore coolies are searched at most inopportune moments. There are a good many Mahomedans in Ghazipur, and they would all like a little opium. The pots after emptying are smashed up and scraped, and heaved down the steep river bank of the factory, where they help to keep the Ganges in its place, so many are they, and the little earthen bowls in which the opium cakes are made. People are forbidden to wander about the river front of the factory in search of remnants of opium on the strands. There are no remnants, but people will not credit this. After vatting, as has been said, the big vats, holding from one to three thousand maunds, are probed with test rods, and the samples are treated just like the samples of the *challans*, everybody writing everything in duplicate and signing it. Having secured the mean consistence of each vat. the requisite quantity of each blend—Calcutta Mint scales again, and an unlimited quantity of supervision—is weighed out, thrown into an alligation vat, of 250 maunds, and worked up by the feet of coolies, who hang on to ropes and drag their legs painfully through the probe. Try to wade in mud of 70° consistency, and see what it is like.

This completes the working of the opium. It is now ready to be made into cakes after a final assay. Man has done nothing to improve it since it streaked the capsule of the poppy—this mysterious drug. Perhaps half a hundred sinners have tried to adulterate it and been paid out accordingly, but that has been the utmost. April, May and June are the months for receiving and manufacturing opium, and in the winter months come the packing and the dispatch.

At the beginning of the cold weather Ghazipur holds locked up a trifle, say, of three and a half millions sterling in opium. Now, there may be only a paltry three-quarters of a million on hand, and that is going out at the rate of one Viceroy's salary for two and a half years per diem. For such a flea-bite it seems absurd to prohibit smoking in the factory or to stud the place with tanks and steam fire-engines. Really, Ghazipur is unnecessarily timid. A long time ago some one threatened to cast down a tree sacred to Mahadeo. In a very few days, just as soon as Mahadeo got news of the insult, a fire broke out and damaged thousands of pounds' worth of opium.

But all this time we have not gone through the factory. There are ranges and ranges of gigantic godowns, huge barns that can hold over half-a-million pounds' worth of opium. There are acres of bricked floor, regiments on regiments of chests; and yet more godowns and more godowns. The heart of the whole is the laboratory which is full of the sick faint smell of a *chandu-khana.* This makes Ghazipur indignant. "That's the smell of opium. We don't need *chandu* here. You don't know what real opium smells like. *Chandu-khana* indeed! That's refined opium under treatment for morphia, and *cocaine* and perhaps *narcoine.*" "Very well, let's see some of the real opium made for the China market." "We shan't be making any for another six weeks at earliest; but we can show you one cake made, and you must imagine two hundred and fifty men making 'em as hard as they can up to one every four minutes." A *Sirdar* of cake-makers is called, and appears with a miniature *dhobi's* washing board on which he sits, a little square box of dark wood, a tin cup, an earthen bowl, and a mass of poppy petal *chupattis.* A larger earthen bowl holds a mass of what looks like bad Cape tobacco. "What's that?" "Trash—dried poppy leaves, not petals, broken up and used for packing cakes in. You'll see presently." The cake-maker sits down and receives a lump of opium, weighed out, of one seer seven chittacks and a half, neither more nor less. "That's pure opium of seventy consistence." Every allowance is weighed. "What are they weighing that brown water for?" "That's *lewa*—thin opium at fifty consistence. It's the paste. He gets four chittacks and a half." "And do they weigh the *chupattis?*" "Of course. Five chittacks of *chupattis*—about sixteen *chupattis* of all three kinds." This is overwhelming. This *sirdar* takes a brass hemispherical cup and wets it with a rag. Then he tears a *chupatti* across so that it fits into the cup without a wrinkle, and pastes it with the thin opium, the *lewa*. After this his actions become incomprehensible, but there is evidently a deep method in them. *Chupatti* after *chupatti* is torn across, dressed with *lewa* and pressed down into the cup, the fringes hanging over the edge of the bowl. He takes half *chupattis* and fixes them skilfully, picking now first-class and now second-class ones. Everything is gummed into everything else with the *lewa*, and he presses all down by twisting his wrists inside the bowl. "He is making the *gattia* now." *Gattia* means a tight coat at any rate, so there is some ray of enlightenment. Torn *chupatti* follows torn *chupatti*, till the bowl is lined half-an-inch deep with them, and they all glisten with the greasy *lewa*. He now takes up an ungummed *chupatti* and fits in carefully all round. The opium is dropped tenderly upon this, and a curious washing motion of the hand follows. The opium is drawn up into a cone as one by one the *sirdar* picks up the overlapping portions of the *chupattis* that hung outside the bowl and plasters them against the drug. He makes a clever waist-belt while he keeps all the flags in place, and so strengthens the midriff of the lump. He tucks in the top of the cone with his thumbs, brings the fringe of *chupattis* over to close the opening, and pastes fresh leaves upon all. The cone has now taken a spherical shape, and he gives it the finishing touch by gumming a large *chupatti*, one of the "moon" kind, set aside from the first, on the top, so deftly that no wrinkle is visible. The cake is now complete, and all the Celestials of the middle kingdom shall not be able to disprove that it weighs two seers one and three-quarter chittacks, with a play of half a chittack for the personal equation.

The Sirdar takes it up and rubs it in the bran-like poppy trash in the big bowl, so that two-thirds of it are powdered with the trash and one-third is fair and shiny *chupatti*. "That is the difference between a Ghazipur and a Patna cake. Our cakes have always an unpowdered head. The Patna ones are rolled in trash all over. You can tell them anywhere by that mark. Now we'll cut this one open and you can see how a section looks." One half of an inch as nearly as may be is the thickness of the *chupatti* shell all round the cake, and even in this short time so firmly has the *lewa* set that any attempt at sundering the skins of *chupatti* is followed by the rending of the poppy petals that compose the *chupatti.* "You've seen in detail what a cake is made of—that is to say, pure opium 70 consistence, poppy-petal pancakes, *lewa*, of 52'-50 consistence, and a powdering of poppy-trash."

"But why are you so particular about the shell?"

"Because of the China market. The Chinaman likes every inch of the stuff we send him, and uses it. He boils the shell and gets out every grain of the *lewa* used to gum it together. He smokes that after he has dried it. Roughly speaking, the value of the cake we've just cut open is two pound ten. All the time it is in our hands we have to look after it and check it, and treat it as though it were gold. It mustn't have too much moisture in it, or it will swell and crack, and if it is too dry John Chinaman won't have it. He values his opium for qualities just the opposite of those in Smyrna opium. Smyrna opium gives as much as ten per cent. of morphia, and is nearly solid—90 consistence. Our opium does not give more than three or three and a half per cent. of morphia on the average, and, as you know it is only 70 or in Patna 75 consistence. That is the drug the Chinaman likes. He can get the maximum of extract out of it by soaking it in hot water, and he likes the flavor. He knows it is absolutely pure too, and it comes to him in good condition." "But has nobody found out any patent way of making these cakes and putting skins on them by machinery?" "Not *yet*. Poppy to poppy. There's nothing better. Here are a couple of cakes made in 1849, when they tried experiments in wrapping them in paper and cloth. You can see that they are beautifully wrapped and sewn like cricket balls, but it would take about half-an-hour to make such cakes, and we could not be sure of keeping the aroma in them. Nothing like poppy plant for poppy drug."

And this is the way the drug, which yields such a splendid income to the Indian Government, is prepared. To tell how it is thereafter kept in store, packed for export, put upon the market at certain fixed periods, and shipped away, for John Chinaman's consumption chiefly, would be a tame story. The interest lies in the actual manufacture and manipulation of the cakes, and we have seen how this is done in the busy factory at Ghazipur.

THE END.

www.ingramcontent.com/pod-product-compliance
Ingram Content Group UK Ltd.
Pitfield, Milton Keynes, MK11 3LW, UK
UKHW012247290726
14090UKWH00013B/507

9 781589 632592